"It's a little weird, you know," Jessica said. "You hung out with Evan after school, like, every night last week, then went on that weird little pseudo-date to the movie yesterday, and now you don't have time to talk to him?"

Elizabeth flinched. "It wasn't a *date*," she said. "Pseudo or whatever. We were just hanging out. As friends." She knew how lame that sounded, and she could tell by the way Jessica's eyes were narrowing that her sister wasn't buying it. "And I really didn't have time to talk today," she insisted. "I had tons of homework."

"Oh, homework, sure," Jessica said. "That's a good excuse. At least, it would have been a year ago."

"What's that supposed to mean?"

"I think it's pretty obvious," Jessica stated. "You're avoiding the guy. And I don't know why you would if you're really *just friends*."

Don't miss any of the books in SWEET VALLEY HIGH
SENIOR YEAR, an exciting series from Bantam Books!

Visit the Official Sweet Valley Web Site on the Internet at:

www.sweetvalley.com

Pascal's
senioryear

BANTAM BOOKS
NEW YORK • TORONTO • LONDON • SYDNEY • AUCKLAND

RL: 6, AGES 012 AND UP

FALLING APART

A Bantam Book / November 2000

Sweet Valley High® is a registered trademark of Francine Pascal.
Conceived by Francine Pascal.
Cover photography by Michael Segal.

Copyright © 2000 by Francine Pascal.
Cover art copyright © 2000 by 17th Street Productions,
an Alloy Online, Inc. company.

 Produced by 17th Street Productions,
an Alloy Online, Inc. company.
33 West 17th Street
New York, NY 10011.

ISBN: 0-553-49339-6

Visit us on the Web! www.randomhouse.com/teens

Published simultaneously in the United States and Canada

Bantam Books is an imprint of Random House Children's Books, a
division of Random House, Inc. BANTAM BOOKS and the rooster
colophon are registered trademarks of Random House, Inc. Bantam Books,
1540 Broadway, New York, New York 10036.

PRINTED IN THE UNITED STATES OF AMERICA

OPM   0 9 8 7 6 5 4 3 2 1

To Susan Johansson

Elizabeth Wakefield

When I was a freshman, I thought the seniors seemed completely in control. I couldn't wait to feel that way. What a joke. Now that I'm a senior, my life is a bigger mess than ever. My sister is acting weird, Tia's furious at me, and my boyfriend—an alcoholic—took off, after making it clear he can't stand to even look at me anymore. Oh, and last night I kissed one of his best friends.

Yeah, things are really pulling together for me this year.

Will Simmons

Not many people can pinpoint the exact second their lives got flushed down the toilet. How did I get so lucky?

Conner McDermott

It's pretty amazing. Now that no one's around to bug me all the time, life sure is easy.

CHAPTER

Total Freedom

1

Conner McDermott jerked awake as a car barreled down the street outside, rattling the window above his head. He blinked, instantly aware that he wasn't in his own bed. The pillow under his cheek was too thin, and the upholstery on the lumpy cushions he was lying on scratched his arms.

Then his head cleared. He was on his father's cheap plaid couch. In his father's tiny, run-down house.

Without lifting his head, he squinted across the living room at the open door of his father's bedroom. The bed was empty, the sheets and blankets spilling onto the floor. He turned to look into the tiny kitchen. Empty too. Conner cocked his head, listening for any sounds from the bathroom. Nothing. He glanced at the clock. Twelve-thirty. *Wow.* He was surprised he'd slept so late in a strange house. Maybe it had to do with the dull thud of a headache he could already feel forming at the back of his skull.

The stale scent of cigarette smoke still hung in

the room. His dad had smoked at least a pack while they were out to dinner last night. But where was he now? His son was visiting, and he took off without waking him up?

He must have left to get us some breakfast, Conner figured.

He yawned and stretched his arms high over his head. Then he piled the blankets at one side of the couch and grabbed the TV remote off the stained coffee table. He switched it on, quickly running through the few channels.

It was difficult to see the screen with the afternoon sun blazing in the picture window behind the couch, but it wasn't like he was into the TV anyway. His dad didn't even have cable. He flipped back and forth between a golf match and a real-estate show.

The female host with the insanely wide smile had shown videos of four houses when Conner started to wonder when his dad was coming back. Picking up some doughnuts shouldn't have taken this long. Even if he'd left just before Conner got up, he should have been back by now.

Conner glared at the TV. That real-estate woman was really getting under his skin. Her polyester power suit and teased hair reminded Conner of all the snotty doctors' wives at his mother's club.

"This next property is quite a charmer," Conner mimicked in a falsetto voice. "It comes complete with two-point-five children, a blue minivan, and the ghost of an ax murderer."

Or maybe the ghost of a deadbeat father who couldn't even bother to spend a whole weekend with his long-lost son, he couldn't help thinking. He ran his hands through his sleep-tousled hair. Apparently spending more than a couple of hours with Conner was too much of a commitment for dear old *Dad.*

Conner had spent Friday night and all day Saturday alone at the house while his dad worked. He'd been starting to think the two of them would never spend any time together, but then Mr. McDermott had taken him out for dinner last night. They hadn't really had much to talk about, but after his father sprang for some drinks, they got along fine. Conner was thinking maybe they could do something today, like check out the rest of Red Bluff, the town where his old man had spent the eleven years since Conner'd last seen him. But now his dad was missing—again.

Disgusted, he punched off the power button on the remote and tossed it onto the floor. It landed under the ratty chair across from the sofa. Conner shrugged. He'd pick it up later.

Shoving himself up, he shuffled into the kitchen and yanked open the fridge. The glaring light inside showed an open can of refried beans, a bag of limp carrots, and a half-empty carton of beer. Conner reached for a can, then hesitated.

3

What the hell, he decided, grabbing one. It wasn't like anyone was around to tell him not to.

He moved to the small set of cupboards over the counter and peered inside. They were empty too except for a container of salt, two cans of tomato soup, and an old package of beef jerky that looked like it had been opened five years ago. Conner shuddered. He wasn't that hungry.

On the counter next to the stove he spotted an open package of tortilla chips. He leaned back against the counter, sipping the beer and munching on some stale chips. Some happy father-son reunion breakfast this was.

Like he should have expected, what, homemade pancakes and fresh-squeezed orange juice? From a man who couldn't be bothered to call his only son in over a decade?

Yeah, right.

He tilted back his head and drained half the beer in one swallow. And then it hit him. He slammed the can down on the counter and laughed out loud. He'd been missing the point entirely. This was a *perfect* situation.

Sometimes half a can of beer is just the thing to set you straight.

He'd left Sweet Valley to get away from everyone else's lame expectations and found a father who gave him total freedom. The man even bought him drinks.

So there was no problem, right? No reason he shouldn't be completely satisfied with the way things were working out for him here.

The last tortilla chip stuck in his throat as he tried to swallow. He balled up the empty bag in his fists and let it sail toward the trash can.

"One double nonfat mocha, no whipped cream," Jeremy Aames announced. He slid the coffee across the counter to the petite woman waiting on the other side. "Have a nice day," he added politely.

The woman smiled and took her drink, then walked over to a small table in the back. Luckily there weren't any customers behind her, which meant Jeremy had a couple of seconds to himself. He glanced up at the clock. One o'clock—a little early for the after-lunch lull at House of Java but definitely not too early to call Jade.

And calling Jade was exactly what he'd been waiting to do ever since he got home from their ultra-confusing date last night. Jade had made it pretty clear a while ago that she wasn't looking for a serious relationship—dating for her was all about fun. At first he hadn't thought he could handle that, but he'd been starting to see how it made life easier. Then last night, after he'd finally decided he knew what was going on with them, she'd shocked him again with The Card incident.

Jeremy shook his head. When she'd talked about

5

going out to celebrate their two-week anniversary, he'd assumed she was kidding. How could the queen of antimush be serious about something like that? But then at the end of the date she'd given him that sweet, *serious* card. All about how happy she was to have him as a *boyfriend*. And he'd given her a completely stupid card making a joke out of the whole night. He felt like such an idiot, and he couldn't wait to talk to her and see what she was really thinking.

Frustrated, he yanked the coffee filter out of the espresso machine and banged it on the side of the plastic trash can to dump out the grounds.

The bells on the front door jangled, and Jeremy looked up to see a shock of green, spiky hair. It was his coworker, Corey Scott, sauntering in from her third cigarette break of the morning. When she finally made it to the counter, Jeremy headed for the back office.

"Break time," he announced without even meeting her eye.

If he didn't grab the chance now, Corey would take off in another two minutes. As far as Jeremy could tell, her entire workday consisted of breaks with as little work as possible in between. If Ally, the manager, hadn't been her sister, she wouldn't have held on to her job for five minutes.

He closed the door of the employee lounge, flopped down on the worn velvet couch, and then dialed Jade's number on Ally's Princess phone.

It rang a couple of times, and then Jade's answering machine picked up. "You've reached the Wus'," her mother's melodic voice stated. "Leave us a message, and we'll call you back."

Jeremy sighed. *Great.* He really wanted to talk to Jade. He couldn't imagine how she'd felt after reading his stupid we're-just-buddies card. He definitely didn't want to leave her with the wrong impression. Whatever that was. What impression did he *want* her to have anyway? He'd spent the whole morning wondering what she actually wanted, but he hadn't even thought about what *he* was looking for here.

He gripped the receiver, trying to figure out the least-lame message possible. When her machine finally beeped, he was completely caught off guard.

"Um, Jade?" he said, licking his lips. "It's Jeremy. I'm at work. House of Java. Well, obviously you know where I work, but—" He stopped, taking a quick breath. "Anyway, you can call me here if you want. My shift doesn't end until four."

He hung up, then leaned his head back on the couch, letting out a low groan. Why exactly had he thought casual dating would be easy?

Elizabeth frowned at the question glowing at the top of her computer screen.

Would Macbeth have made a good leader? Why or why not?

She sighed. She was *not* in the mood for AP

7

English homework, but it was Sunday afternoon, and the assignment was due in the morning.

Macbeth would definitely not have been a good leader, she typed. *He had way too many problems to pay much attention to anybody else. Not a good quality in a king. He's much more the flawed-hero type.*

Her hands dropped from the keyboard. *A flawed hero. Like Conner.* Not that Conner was exactly a hero. But he *was* flawed.

What was the matter with her? Did everything in the universe really have to relate to Conner McDermott in her mush of a brain?

"Hey, Liz," Steven, her brother, called up the stairs. He was home from college for the weekend. "Evan's on the phone for you."

Her body stiffened slightly at the sound of Evan's name. He'd already called once earlier that morning, and she'd avoided talking to him. After last night she didn't have any idea what to say to him.

Sorry, I didn't mean to kiss you.

Sorry I made you think that I wanted to kiss you.

Sorry, you're my boyfriend's friend and so I can never, ever kiss you again.

No, it was definitely easier to avoid him for a while. Although as stupid as it sounded, she already missed Evan after going just one morning without talking to him. The past week he'd been everywhere she was—listening, supporting, just doing whatever she needed while Conner was away. And she'd had a great time with him at the movie yesterday. It had all been fine until they'd pulled up to her house and he'd leaned across her to get her door open, brushing against her—

"Hey, Liz-ard," Steven yelled up again. "Te-le-phone."

Elizabeth shoved back her chair and stumbled toward the door. She couldn't talk to Evan right now. Not until she figured out what she felt. Or what she should feel.

She hurried down the stairs and whirled around the corner toward the kitchen, figuring she'd just tell Steven to let Evan know she wasn't home. Her brother was standing in front of the counter, drinking the leftover milk from his cereal bowl. The receiver sat on the counter next to him. She tried to motion to him to come away from the phone, but with the big bowl in front of his face, he didn't see her. Before she could stop him, he'd put down the empty bowl and grabbed the basketball sitting next to the cereal box. Then he took off out the back door.

Elizabeth wished he'd left the ball there. She would have loved to bounce it off the back of his big, fat head.

She stared down at the phone. Now she was stuck.

Or maybe not.

The idea that flashed through her brain was completely absurd. Not to mention cruel and immature.

9

But it beat fumbling through a conversation with Evan.

Just do it, she told herself. *Just grab the phone and go for it.*

Gingerly she reached down and picked up the receiver. She cleared her throat. "Hi, Evan, it's Jessica," she said in her best imitation of her twin's slightly higher-pitched voice.

Silence.

"Jess?" He sounded a little confused, but at least he hadn't called her bluff instantly. "Wow," he finally said. "You, um—you sounded like your sister."

Elizabeth coughed. "Mmmm," she responded. "No, it's me."

"Oh," he said. He paused. "Well, actually, I was calling for Liz. Is she around?"

"No, sorry," she replied, making sure to keep her tone breezy and light, like Jessica's. "Library, I think," she continued. Somehow she felt like the fewer words she uttered, the more likely he was to buy that she was really Jessica.

"Oh, okay," Evan said, his disappointment obvious. Elizabeth cringed. She couldn't help feeling happy that he wanted to talk to her that badly, but she *knew* that wasn't right. "Well, could you just tell her I called?"

Elizabeth's fingers relaxed around the receiver. "Sure."

"Great. Thanks, Jess."

"No problem," she said with relief, hanging up.

She sank down into a chair at the kitchen table, shaking her head. When was the last time she and Jessica had pulled something like that, trying to switch places? She knew even just doing it over the phone was really unfair. But not as unfair as having to give Evan an explanation when she simply didn't have one.

Conner stepped out of the bathroom, rubbing his hair dry with a towel he'd found in his dad's room. He paused, surveying the messy living room. It was even worse than his bedroom.

Conner folded the towel loosely over his arm and draped it on the edge of the sofa. He'd gone for a quick ride to the store before his shower to pick up some juice. He wasn't really sure what to do now, though. Maybe watch some more bad TV.

Just then the front door swung open and Mr. McDermott walked inside the house. He stopped when he saw Conner. "Oh," he said, frowning. "I thought you took off or something. I didn't see your car."

"Yeah, I left it around the corner," Conner explained, shifting his weight from one foot to the other. From the sour expression on his dad's face, it seemed like he'd actually been *hoping* Conner wouldn't be around.

"Baby, I've gotta use the little girls' room before I

11

just *die*," a high-pitched voice whined from behind Conner's dad.

Conner blinked.

A slender woman with bleached blond hair squeezed around Mr. McDermott into the house. Conner's eyebrows shot up as he took in her short shorts, tight pink T-shirt, and layers of makeup. She was dressed like some tacky girl from his school—not like a woman his *dad's* age.

She gave Conner a coy smile as she passed him. "'Scuze me, honey," she said, scooting into the bathroom and shutting the door behind her.

He glanced back at his dad, waiting for him to say something. But instead of explaining who the woman was, Mr. McDermott just crossed over to the TV and switched it on, then sank down on the couch. "I'm gonna watch the game," he mumbled.

Conner stood still for a moment, then walked over to grab his wallet from the coffee table, sticking it in the back pocket of his jeans. At least he'd gotten dressed in the bathroom, so he hadn't had to face his dad's little girlfriend in just a towel.

The toilet flushed, and Conner could hear water running through the old pipes. A second later the woman emerged from the bathroom.

"Hey, Wanda, get me a beer, would you?" his father said, never taking his eyes off the TV.

That was it. No, "Hey, Wanda, let me introduce you to my son." Wasn't Wanda at all curious about

12

who this guy standing in the living room was? Unless Mr. McDermott had already filled her in. Told her how much he wished Conner hadn't showed up here.

Anger and humiliation burned in his stomach, but he forced himself to keep his expression as blank as his dad's.

Wanda headed for the kitchen, her platform shoes clicking on the floor. Underneath all the makeup she looked easily old enough to be his mother. Except his mother didn't wear shorts small enough for her butt to hang out the back.

Wanda opened the fridge, then glanced back at Conner. "You want one, sweetie?" she asked him.

He shook his head. "No, thanks."

It was past time for him to get out of here. His father clearly wanted to be alone with Wanda the bimbo. Which was fine by him. Solo time was exactly what he'd been craving lately. Conner grabbed his car keys off the counter and headed for the front door.

His hand was on the doorknob when his father made a gargled noise that sounded like an attempt to clear his throat. "Hey, where's the remote?" he called out.

Conner glanced at the small gray box on the floor, wedged under the chair. "No idea," he replied with a shrug.

He yanked open the door and headed across the

overgrown lawn. His dad hadn't even asked where he was going, when he'd be back—

Am I losing it here? Conner wondered, running a hand through his damp hair. *Finally* no one was questioning his every move, and he couldn't just be happy with that?

He strolled down the block and around the corner to where he'd left his Mustang just under an hour ago. He unlocked the door, hopped in, and turned the key in the ignition. The engine caught with a deep rumble. *Like always.* He fingered the shift lever, his foot heavy on the accelerator. The huge engine growled, shaking the car. The power felt good. Great, actually.

He gunned the engine and roared past his father's house. Just to let the guy know he was glad to be out of that stinking place.

The fuel tank was still three-quarters full. Plenty of gas to put a zillion miles between him and his lame excuse for a father. Only he had no idea where to head. And he didn't have the energy to think about it. So he just cruised up and down the streets of his father's seedy neighborhood.

With each dilapidated house he passed, Conner felt worse. He'd spent the past eleven years wondering where his dad was, what he was up to, and he'd never imagined such a pathetic neighborhood or the lame, menial job his dad worked. Not to mention his bimbo girlfriend.

Conner gunned the car around a corner, making the tires squeal. He passed a deserted-looking strip mall. The kind where all the stores had gates that slid across the windows at night. He drove on, just following the road until it started to wind up a hill. He had to pay more attention to his driving, which wasn't such a bad thing, considering his thoughts were pretty damn depressing.

Just when he was getting tired of the hairpin turns, the road came up to a county park with a parking lot right beside a small river. Conner pulled over and parked, then got out and walked down a grassy hill to the edge of the water. He sat down on the grass and pulled his legs up to his chest. The afternoon sun felt warm and soothing on his skin. He arched into the warmth, watching the water rippling over the boulders in the river.

His stomach didn't hurt anymore, he realized. It seemed like the more distance he put between himself and his father, the better he felt. But then, the more distance he put between himself and everybody in his life lately, the better he felt.

Unable to stop himself, in his thoughts he drifted back to the scene he'd found in his house only a few days ago. His friends, Elizabeth, his mom, his *sister* . . . all of them waiting there to ambush him about his "problem." Why all of a sudden had every single person in his life decided to jump on his back and drive him away?

Even Liz.

He plucked a blade of grass and shredded it between his fingers. If she'd just let it go, then he wouldn't be here right now. The two of them would be together, and then somehow everything would be okay—the way it always seemed like it could be when she was around.

Only it wasn't. Clearly his life was flying apart at the speed of light; otherwise he wouldn't be thinking cheesy thoughts about how Elizabeth could just make the world go happily around.

A bird called somewhere off to his left. He turned his head to look and then groaned in pain. The muscles in his neck had pulled so tight, they felt like steel bands. He closed his eyes and slowly, gingerly tried to rotate his head to unknot the muscles.

What he really needed right now wasn't Elizabeth Wakefield—it was a drink. No, he didn't *need* it. He didn't need anything. But he wanted a drink, wanted it so badly, the taste of the alcohol burning his lips and his throat was almost real. A drink would calm him down, ease up the tightness in his muscles. It would slow down the thoughts whipping through his head.

Yeah, he wanted a drink. No—several. Too bad he hadn't taken Wanda up on her beer offer.

Then he stiffened, remembering. There was still a bottle of vodka in his trunk. He'd stashed it there the other day, when he'd had to pick Megan up from the mall.

16

For the first time that day he grinned. That was what he needed: some liquid relaxation. That would put his head back on straight.

He stood up, pulled his keys out of his pants pocket, and took off toward his car.

Jessica Wakefield

To: lizw@cal.rr.com, tee@swiftnet.com, mslater@swiftnet.com
From: jess1@cal.rr.com
Time: 4:56 P.M.
Subject: Homecoming dance—what else!

Hey, you guys—

I'm totally psyched you're all on the homecoming-dance committee with me!! I mean, this is it—our senior year—our <u>last</u> homecoming dance. This is gonna be <u>so</u> fun.

I was thinking: What if we get together after cheering practice on Thursday and make the posters for the dance? Oh, and everybody think of ideas, okay? I thought the posters the seniors did last year were beyond lame.

And I think everybody's going to try and meet at lunch on Friday to start decorating the gym. That way we won't have so much to do Friday after school. Maybe some of us could even get out of sixth and seventh periods to decorate?

I wouldn't mind that. :)

Later,

Jess

Jade Wu

I think one of the worst things in the world is to be <u>pitied.</u> It's worse than not even being liked at all. And from the sound of Jeremy's voice on my machine, he took one look at that stupid card I gave him and immediately felt sorry for me.

Ugh.

I just have to make it very clear to him that I didn't mean a word of it, and then he won't feel so bad about not wanting to be my boyfriend. It's not like it should be hard—I've done this a million times before.

Only one small difference—I actually care about Jeremy. A lot.

CHAPTER 2

No. Yes. Okay, Maybe.

Melissa Fox flopped back on her bed and set the phone on her stomach. She sighed, trying to prepare herself for another gloomy conversation with Will. Ever since he'd gotten home from the hospital, he'd been more bitter every time she talked to him. And he was still refusing to see her.

She took a deep breath, then dialed his number. *Maybe today he'll be doing better,* she told herself.

The phone rang a few times before Will picked up. "Yeah?" he grunted, his voice sounding kind of heavy.

Melissa cringed. Just that one syllable told her everything she needed to know.

"Hey," she said, struggling to sound normal.

"What's going on?" he asked, sounding like he couldn't possibly be less interested in her reply. She wondered why he bothered to ask at all.

"Nothing," she responded. She bit her lip. He could at least *sound* happy to hear from her.

Lifting her chin slightly, she scooted up on the bed until her back was resting against the headboard.

Maybe she just needed to try harder to get him pumped up. She *was* a cheerleader. "Guess what I heard?" she said, forcing excitement into her voice. "You know Mike Petro from Big Mesa? Gina told me he totaled his Explorer last night. I guess he's okay and everything, but his SUV is history."

"Huh," Will answered. "At least he can still drive."

"Well, yeah," Melissa said, wincing. She'd thought that stupid gossip about people he knew from the outside world could get his mind off himself, but of course she'd just made things worse. She twirled the phone cord around her fingers, racking her mind for something else. "Did the doctor say you could come back to school yet?" she blurted out.

Will didn't say anything at first, and she heard a strange staticky sound, like he was playing with the Velcro straps on his knee brace. "He said whenever I feel ready," Will finally said.

"That's great!" She sat forward, instantly energized. "Why don't you try this week? You don't even have to stay for—"

"I'm not ready," he cut in.

"But Will, everybody misses you."

He snorted. "Right. Sure."

"What are you talking about? Of course they do," she insisted. *I do,* she added silently. But he didn't seem to care about that.

He sighed. "Look, my knee is really killing me. You don't know what it's like, okay?"

Melissa glared at the photo of Will taped to the mirror above her dresser. How many times had he said that to her lately? She totally got that it was going to be hard coming back to school with everything so different from how it was a few weeks ago. Going from star quarterback to regular guy would suck. God, it wasn't like *she* wasn't dealing with the same type of thing—going from being the star quarterback's *girlfriend* to . . . whatever she was now. And if she could handle it, why couldn't he at least try? He was going to have to do it sometime.

She tucked the phone between her cheek and her shoulder and closed her eyes, trying to keep her frustration from exploding. All she'd do was drive him further away, like after Ken Matthews showed up at the hospital, getting Will so angry that he started refusing to see Melissa and didn't even talk to her for a few days. She'd called his house a million times before he'd finally agreed to talk again.

Just keep it neutral, she thought, easing her grip on the phone. She pasted a smile on her lips, even though he couldn't see her. "So how's the home schooling going?" she asked. "Are you staying on top of things?"

Will made another grunting sound. "I don't know," he mumbled. "I don't get the calculus stuff, and she doesn't really explain it well."

Melissa hesitated. This was the perfect opportunity. "I'm doing okay in that class," she said. "I could help you." She glanced over at the pink-rimmed clock on her desk. "It's only six-thirty," she added. "I could come over now and then maybe stay for dinner or something."

Will was quiet, and she began to hope that she'd finally broken through.

"No," Will said firmly. Like he'd said every single night since the accident. "I don't think that's a good idea."

Melissa wanted to scream. "Will, this is getting pretty ridiculous, don't you think? You won't even let your own girlfriend come see you?" She sighed. "I mean, if this is all about my seeing you on crutches, believe me, I can handle it."

"It's not that simple," he responded, the exasperation obvious in his voice. "Don't you get it?"

Her jaw clenched. "Get what?" she demanded, gritting her teeth. "Are you ever going to—"

"Look, I'm just not *ready* yet."

"Yeah, whatever," she said sharply.

He sighed. "I have to go."

Melissa's throat closed up. "Okay, fine. Bye," she managed to whisper.

"Bye," he said.

The phone clicked in her ear, followed an instant later by the shrill buzz of the dial tone.

The blood went rushing to her head. After everything he'd put her through this year, she'd still been there for him every second since his knee got crushed on the field. But how much longer could she take being treated this way?

Conner stared out at the water. He put his mouth to the bottle and tilted back his head. A tiny drop of liquid splashed on his tongue. He held the bottle up to his ear and shook it.

Not a sound.

Disgusted, he hurled it into the river. There hadn't been enough vodka left to get him very buzzed at all. Not the kind of buzz he needed tonight. He shivered and folded his arms across his chest. Now that the sun was setting, it was getting cold fast.

He stood up, swaying a little as he got to his feet, and headed back across the grass to his Mustang. At least it was a little warmer inside the car. He sure wished he had some more vodka, though. Those couple of swigs had only made his craving worse. And they hadn't even touched the aching muscles in his neck.

His energy level was suddenly sky-high. He drummed his fingers on the steering wheel, feeling increasingly anxious. The longer he sat, the more the pleasant, numbing effects of the alcohol wore off. And the more desperate he got.

He didn't know this town well enough to have an idea where he'd be able to buy some more vodka without a fake ID. There was a great little store back in El Carro where they probably wouldn't have carded a ten-year-old. But here in Red Bluff, he wasn't sure where to go. Then he remembered—they'd served him at that restaurant his father took him to last night. The bartender hadn't even blinked when his dad had bought rounds for the two of them. So either they believed Conner was over twenty-one, or they didn't care. Both options worked for him.

Conner noticed his hand shook slightly as he turned the key in the ignition, probably from all the nervous energy running through his body. He tore out of the parking lot and headed back down the hill toward town.

The winding road was still deserted. Did anyone live here besides his dad and Wanda? Conner stepped on the gas, blown away by how well the Mustang accelerated through the banked curves. He rested his left elbow on the door frame, smiling to himself. A hard curve loomed up suddenly, and he took it a little wide, letting the car drift onto the gravel shoulder. He jerked the wheel back too quickly, making the back wheels fishtail. The car came back under control, but Conner's heart was pounding. In the rearview window he could see the cloud of dust the car had kicked up.

He blinked, his pulse racing. These roads really were dangerous. Drivers probably had those near misses all the time around here. He leaned forward, fingers clenching the wheel in a death grip, and concentrated on keeping the car in the very center of his lane the rest of the way down the hill.

There was only a handful of cars in the restaurant's parking lot when he pulled in. *Damn.* He had hoped it would be busier. That way he'd blend in better.

Oh, well. Hopefully the same people from last night would be working, and if they recognized him, he didn't expect a problem. The waitress had seemed to know his dad pretty well.

He swung into a parking spot, then headed over to the building. There were two entrances, one to the bar and the other to the main restaurant. Quickly he decided to go straight for the bar, hoping it would make him look more like he knew what he was doing.

He hesitated, his hand around the door handle. What if it didn't work? Then he shrugged. What if it didn't? They'd laugh in his face and tell him to get out. That's what. Big deal. Nothing to lose, really.

Still, he was glad he could still feel some of the effects of the vodka he'd downed. It took the edge off, made him stress out less. He pulled open the door, and the familiar scents of cigarette smoke and beer hit him. He strode in, trying to keep his muscles relaxed and walk with that confident, I-do-this-all-the-time kind of stride.

The interior was dim and smoky, like a dark, comforting cave. The only people in the bar section were an older couple sharing a pitcher of beer at a corner table next to the gaudy jukebox. The same bartender that had been on duty the other night was drying wineglasses and hanging them upside down on a rack over the bar. Perfect. The guy glanced over at Conner and smiled. Conner lifted his chin in a nonchalant greeting.

The bartender put up the last wineglass. "What can I get you?"

"Vodka rocks," he said quickly, as if the man would change his mind any second about serving him.

The bartender nodded and set up Conner's drink, then he moved back to the other end of the bar and started washing glasses in the tiny sink.

Conner knocked back half the drink in one gulp, then glanced around cautiously, worried that he'd seem too eager. But the couple in the corner were staring into each other's eyes, and the bartender was busy washing up.

Absently Conner watched him work. The slug of vodka seemed to hit his brain in an instant. The tension melted out of his muscles. Just what he needed, he thought with satisfaction. He drained the glass and occupied himself with eating nuts out of the bowl in front of him until the bartender looked his way again.

" 'Nother one?" the bartender asked.

His mouth full of peanuts, Conner nodded.

He drank the second one even faster. On top of what he'd already had, the alcohol went straight to his head. If he closed his eyes, he felt like the room was spinning ever so slightly. The music from the speakers above the bar seemed to undulate in waves of sound, getting louder, then softer, then louder again.

Conner was dimly aware that more people had come in. He could hear the low level of conversation. Some guy laughed, a loud burst that sounded just like Evan.

An image of his friend entered his head—the look on Evan's face when he tried to convince Conner not to climb that rock at Crescent Beach, the night he ended up falling. A strange well of emotion filled his chest, for no good reason.

Fighting for composure, he focused hard on the bottles lined up across the back bar. He named each one in his head, trying to push away thoughts of anyone back home.

The answer is: more booze, he decided.

He sat up straight and gripped the padded edge of the bar, giving his head a small shake to try and get rid of that clouded feeling. He knew he wouldn't get served if he seemed like the alcohol was starting to get to him. He lifted his hand to signal the bartender. When he caught the man's attention, he put up two fingers.

The bartender lifted his eyebrows in surprise, but a minute later he set two more drinks in front of Conner.

The first drink made him even dizzier, but he

could still *think*—could still see Evan's *concerned,* disapproving expression. So he quickly downed the liquid in the second glass too. Then the music in the background caught his attention. A familiar guitar riff exploded through his brain, sending him back to the safety of his room, where he'd practiced the same amazing riffs until his fingers were practically blistered. *Carlos Santana, the God of Guitar.* He closed his eyes, letting the master's rhythms carry him out of his own screwed-up head.

Until it all came to a crashing halt.

One minute he was onstage, playing backup on "Soul Sacrifice," the next, some twangy, country-western crap was blaring from behind him, drowning out everything else and exploding the cocoon of comfort around him.

Before he was even aware of it, Conner had spun around on the bar stool and stood up. He glared in the direction of the sound. Through a fuzzy haze he saw a tall guy in a cowboy hat leaning over the jukebox.

He staggered forward, tripping over a chair and almost falling before he caught himself on an empty table. "What the hell—," he yelled.

The cowboy's eyes flickered over Conner, then his lip curled in disgust. "Can I help you?" he spat out.

The closer Conner got, the blurrier the man's outline became. The stupid country song vibrated through his head, feeding the rage inside him.

"I'm listening to a song. Turn that crap off," he demanded.

The cowboy laughed and crossed his arms over his chest. "You gonna make me?"

Conner leaped forward, his fist raised. "You bet," he said, then took a swing. He missed completely and ended up catching himself on the side of the jukebox.

"Okay, that's enough," a rough voice behind Conner commanded.

An instant later a fist tangled itself in the front of his shirt and he found himself being pulled across the floor.

"Stay put so I don't have to hurt you," the man—he thought maybe it was the bartender—growled in his face. He threw him into a booth and walked away.

Conner glared at the man's back. *Shut up,* he thought, but he wasn't sure the words actually made it out of his mouth around his thick tongue.

He tried to look around, blinking a couple of times, but the room remained a blur. Lights trailed off into squiggly white lines. It seemed like the slower he moved his head, the faster the room bucked around. He closed his eyes, but it didn't help. His stomach heaved up into his throat.

He laid his cheek against the cool tabletop and wrapped his arms protectively around his head. He wasn't asleep, exactly, but he wasn't awake either. All he knew was his head was spinning out of control and everything inside him felt about to come up. Nothing else existed. He stayed like that, unable to move, for what felt like days.

Until he felt someone shaking his shoulder.

"Conner, get up," a voice said from above him.

He raised his head and blinked in shock. His father glared down at him.

"Let's go," Mr. McDermott said. He pulled Conner up by his arm and dragged him through the bar.

Something banged against Conner's shin. "Ouch," he yelped.

His father kept right on moving, towing him along out the door. He shoved Conner into the front seat of a car and slammed the door.

The next instant everything went black.

Elizabeth let out a yawn as she pulled back the covers on her bed, feeling more ready than she ever had for some deep, relaxing sleep. But just as she was about to climb in, Jessica burst into her room.

"I was cleaning off my dresser," Jessica explained, holding out a pair of earrings. "Here are your silver hoops back." When Elizabeth didn't make a move to come grab them, Jessica dropped them on the desk next to her.

"Thanks," Elizabeth said. Usually she had to venture into Jessica's room to track down her things. Usually. Ha. Always. Still, right now the last thing on her mind was retrieving lost jewelry. Now, if Jessica would just turn around and bounce right back *out* of her room . . .

Jessica crossed over and plopped down on the edge of Elizabeth's bed. She paused, running her hand along the blue comforter. "You're sure popular today," she said. "Evan must have called you five times. What's up with that?"

Elizabeth swallowed. She knew that tone. It was Jessica's I'm-pretending-to-sound-uninterested voice. Which meant Jessica sensed there was something going on. She had no idea herself what was happening between her and Evan, let alone the ability to explain it to her twin.

Elizabeth shrugged, hoping she looked more casual than Jessica had sounded. "I don't know. I haven't called him back yet."

The bed squeaked as Jessica leaned forward. "Yeah, I noticed," she said. She swung her head so that her blond ponytail moved back behind her shoulder. "It's a little weird, you know. You hung out with him after school, like, every night last week, then went on that weird little pseudo-date to the movie yesterday, and now you don't have time to talk to him?"

Elizabeth flinched. "It wasn't a *date*," she said. "Pseudo or whatever. We were just hanging out. As friends." She knew how lame that sounded, and she could tell by the way Jessica's eyes were narrowing that her sister wasn't buying it. "And I really didn't have time to talk today," she insisted. "I had tons of homework."

"Oh, homework, sure," Jessica said. "That's a good excuse. At least, it would have been a year ago."

"What's that supposed to mean?" Elizabeth walked over to her desk, picking up the earrings Jessica had left there and moving them over to the jewelry box on her dresser. She kept her back to her sister, afraid to see the expression on her face.

"I think it's pretty obvious," Jessica stated. "You're avoiding the guy. And I don't know why you would if you're really *just friends*."

"I'm not avoiding him," Elizabeth argued, straightening out the chain on her silver heart necklace before shutting the jewelry box.

"Oh, right. I have a personal rule never to call people back until they've left me seven messages too," Jessica said sarcastically.

"I just didn't feel like talking to anybody today," Elizabeth blurted out, turning back around to face her sister. "Is that so terrible?" she added, her voice rising.

Jessica's eyes widened in surprise. She paused, tilting her head to the side. "So there's nothing going on between you and Evan?" she asked.

A picture of the almost-kiss in Evan's car last night flashed through Elizabeth's mind. *No. Yes. Okay, maybe.*

"That's what I thought," Jessica said when Elizabeth didn't answer. A look of disgust came over her features. "What are you going to do, dump Evan the minute Conner gets back? Or are you just going to bail out on Conner, the supposed love of your life until things got a little rough?"

Elizabeth's jaw dropped. How could Jessica be so cruel? "You have no idea what I'm dealing with," she said, tears stinging the back of her eyelids. "You have *no right* to say that to me."

This was all so wrong. Somehow things were making less and less sense to her all the time, and she didn't know how to stop it.

Jessica watched the wet sheen of tears begin to build in her sister's eyes, hardening herself against the natural instinct to comfort her. She hated to see Elizabeth cry, but this time her usually do-gooder sister had stepped over the line.

How could Elizabeth act like this? How could she think she might have feelings for a guy Jessica had dated? Weren't they past all that stuff? Hadn't they grown out of the whole stealing-each-other's-boyfriends phase? And Elizabeth already *had* a boyfriend. Conner hadn't been holding up his end of the deal too well lately, but he had a lot going on. Jessica couldn't believe her twin would turn on him so fast like that—with one of his *friends* too. If this were Jessica, Elizabeth would be laying into her big time.

And besides, she *did* have a right to take this personally. Her own love life was completely nonexistent, and now she had to watch Evan and her sister together? That was too much.

"I really can't believe you're doing this," Jessica said quietly. "It's not like I've ever been a huge Conner fan, but you know, even he deserves better. And Evan *definitely* does."

Elizabeth jerked back as if Jessica had slapped her, and the tears blurred her eyes, obviously about to spill. "Jess, nothing has happened with me and Evan," she said, her voice wavering. "All we've done is hang out. I don't understand why everyone has such a problem with that."

Jessica frowned. "Liz," she said softly, "if that's all there was, then you *wouldn't* be so upset right now."

Elizabeth didn't say anything, and Jessica noticed that she was twisting her hands together in front of her. "I don't have feelings for Evan," she muttered.

"Fine," Jessica said, jumping up from the bed and walking over to stand in front of her sister. "Maybe you don't. But did it ever occur to you that you might be giving him the wrong idea?"

"Did it ever occur to you that you're just jealous?" Elizabeth snapped.

Jessica's eyebrows shot up. "What is the *matter* with you?" she said. "You are acting like a major brat."

Elizabeth held her gaze. "Really?" she said. "Well, then, I guess you wouldn't want a *brat* working with

35

you on the homecoming committee. So count me out." She stepped around Jessica, heading back over to the bed. "Close the door on your way out," she called over her shoulder.

Jessica stormed out of the room, making a point to slam the door behind her.

Will Simmons

Reasons to Go Back to School on Monday

1. Real classes are less boring than home school.
2. I'm sick of daytime TV. Oprah, Montel, and Jerry Springer are lame.
3. My friends.
4. Melissa.

Reasons Not to Start Back to School on Monday

1. Microwave burritos stink less than cafeteria food.
2. No alarm clocks.
3. Having to watch the football team go to practice. Without me.
4. Pity sucks.

To: jess1@cal.rr.com
From: mslater@swiftnet.com
Time: 10:37 P.M.
Subject: re: Homecoming dance

Hi, Jessica—
   Listen, I'm sorry, but I'm not going to stay on the homecoming-dance committee. Homecoming is all about stupid football, and the thought of anything even slightly related to that ridiculous sport makes me sick.
   Don't be mad at me, okay?
                              Maria

CHAPTER 3

Attacked by School Spirit

Andy struggled to keep up with Tia as she dodged the crowds in the hallway on the way to first-period history.

"Did you read that chapter about the gold rush?" Tia asked him over her shoulder. "I thought it would never end."

Andy let out a short laugh. "Yeah, that's why I didn't read it," he replied.

And that's why my grades are hovering right above the toilet, he added to himself. As far as he was concerned, watching grass grow was more interesting than studying.

Tia stopped short, turning to face him with a sharp glare. "Andy! You've barely passed the last three quizzes."

"Good point," he said, frowning. "Can you give me a quick rundown of the chapter on the way to class?"

Tia sighed. "It's an entire chapter of American history," she said, "not a knock-knock joke. It would take me more than five minutes to catch you up."

Andy shifted his backpack higher on his shoulder. "Seriously, even if you could just give me the highlights or some of the names of the major players, you know—" He stopped as a poster from the wall came down right on his head, covering his eyes. "Help! I'm being attacked by school spirit," he joked, reaching up to pull the poster away.

Tia yanked the heavy paper out of his hands, holding it up in front of her.

He took a step back, rubbing his head, then glanced at the big, bold words in red lettering. *Go, Sweet Valley. Homecoming Rules!* There was a crudely painted picture of a guy and a girl dancing next to the words.

Andy slapped his palm against his forehead. "Oh, of course. Homecoming. How could I have forgotten to put *that* on my calendar?"

"Come on, Andy," Tia said, propping the poster against the wall on the floor. She turned and continued heading down the hall, brushing a few strands of her long, dark hair out of her face. "It's just a dance."

Andy jogged a few steps to catch up to her. "You don't sound too psyched about it either," he pointed out.

Tia sighed, quickening her pace a little. He knew she always walked faster when she had something on her mind. After Tia and Angel had just broken up, he practically had to speed walk to keep up with her.

"It's not really the dance," Tia admitted. "It's the

stupid planning committee I'm supposed to be on. I told Jessica I'd do it, but I really don't want to deal. I'm still pretty mad at Liz for all that stuff she said to me the other day."

Andy shrugged. He'd seen Tia right after her fight with Elizabeth, and he knew it had been brutal. "So maybe you should drop out," he suggested. "And skip the dance."

"Yeah, right," Tia muttered.

"No, really," Andy persisted. "It's not like it's mandatory. In fact, according to the SVH rule book, I think the only thing that's mandatory besides attendance and passing grades is staying out of food fights in the cafeteria."

Tia laughed. "I guess you're right," she said. "I don't know; I kept thinking I had to do it."

"Let me put it this way," he began. "I don't think they'll send everyone home early because Tia Ramirez didn't show up."

Tia flashed him a grin. "Okay, I get the idea," she said. She paused. "So why don't we hang out together Friday night? I mean, since everyone else is going to be at the dance, we could have our own fun night."

"And miss the crowning of the homecoming queen? Let me think." Andy scrunched up his nose, pretending to consider it. Then he smiled at her. "Yeah, I'm there." The last few weeks had been pretty high-pressure for him. Telling his friends he was gay and then telling his *parents*. He really wasn't up for the whole school-dance ritual. But a night on the town with Tia—now that she was finally able to listen to *him* talk sometimes instead of just rambling forever about her problems—sounded like exactly what he needed.

They reached the classroom, and Andy held open the door, standing aside so she could go in first. "You know, there is a way you could thank me for helping you see that you don't have to do this homecoming thing," he said as he walked in behind her.

"Oh, really?" Tia replied.

"Yeah—you could start filling me in on that gold-rush stuff," he mumbled.

Tia laughed, but as Andy sat down at his desk, he wished he'd been joking. He really couldn't afford to bomb another quiz. Still, at least he had plans for the night of the homecoming dance now. Homecoming, dances, dating—they were all just reminders that Andy Marsden didn't fit in.

Well, this was one reminder he was happy to skip.

Melissa squinted at Mr. Nelson, the senior-class guidance counselor. He was standing behind the podium at the front of the auditorium, lecturing the seniors on college-admissions procedures.

Cherie Reese tapped her on the arm. "Can you believe he's actually wearing that rug?" she whispered.

"How are we supposed to take somebody like that seriously?"

Melissa wrinkled her nose. "I know. It's tragic."

The girl on Cherie's right passed her a handful of papers. She took one and handed them to Melissa, who passed them on to their other friend, Gina Cho.

Mr. Nelson cleared his throat. "Remember as you read, people, these are the *bare-minimum* requirements for most colleges." He paused to frown meaningfully at the audience. "Just having everything on this list won't guarantee you get into one of the colleges you choose. If you've picked popular schools, you're going to have to show them something special."

No kidding, Melissa thought as she scanned the list. She chewed on her lip. Will hadn't done even half of these things. Now that a football scholarship was out, he was going to have to apply to schools just like a regular student. What kind of shot did he have?

Cherie pulled her thick, auburn curls back off her face with one hand and leaned across Melissa. "He is really freaking me out," she said to Gina.

Gina's dark eyes widened. "I know," she agreed.

Melissa smirked. Gina's grades were pretty pathetic. *Like Will's.* The thought made her stomach clench.

Amy Sutton, who was sitting right behind them, moved forward to join the quiet conversation. "You must feel so lucky," she told Melissa. "I mean, knowing that you and Will are going somewhere together."

Melissa forced herself to smile confidently. *Not anymore,* she thought. Since the night Will got hurt, nothing was the same, nothing was as certain as it had been. Of course, no one knew that. Melissa hadn't told a single one of her friends how serious Will's injury was. That he wouldn't play football again. That his scholarship to Michigan was gone, just like that. People only looked up to you if you had power, and without Will, she wasn't sure how far her power would go.

". . . and I sincerely hope you already have applications from the schools you wish to apply to. If you don't, you need to request them immediately," Mr. Nelson droned on. "The deadlines for most schools are in a couple of weeks."

If Will can even make it into college, Melissa thought bitterly. Her jaw tightened with anger. He'd always been so sure he was going somewhere on a football scholarship, he didn't think schoolwork mattered. Now he probably couldn't get in anywhere.

Panic started to squeeze her chest, so she could barely breathe. She glanced quickly at Cherie, who was staring straight ahead at Mr. Nelson again. No one seemed to have noticed that Melissa's control was slipping, at least.

She doodled slow, swirling curves in the margin of the notebook resting on her lap. Did Will even care what his attitude did to *her* future? She'd changed all her dreams to fit his plans at Michigan. Now that he'd lost that, she'd lost everything too. Couldn't he just for once think about what all this was doing to her?

Mr. Nelson clapped to get everyone's attention. "All right, students. I know this is a lot of information to absorb, so each of you will have an individual appointment with me to go over your admissions packets and discuss your progress. Make sure you check the sheets on the wall on your way out to find out when your appointment is."

Will wasn't going to make it to an appointment. Melissa would bet her lucky varsity cheerleading jacket on it. He couldn't even face coming to school. He was going to stay locked up in his house until it was too late to plan anything for next year. She stuffed the college-prep list in her folder and slammed it shut. Well, *she* wouldn't. She'd waited too long to get out of Sweet Valley. If Will couldn't get his life together, she'd just have to get one of her own.

Conner lay in bed for what seemed like forever before he finally made himself open his eyes.

He immediately wished he hadn't.

White, blinding light made his head pound so hard, he thought it might split apart. He groaned and squeezed his eyes tightly shut again. It didn't help. His head still pulsed with pain.

Still, something felt strange—off. Then it hit him. He was sleeping on his back. He never slept on his back.

Slowly this time, he cracked open his eyes. Even allowing for a hangover, the room was ridiculously bright, so bright, his eyes watered and he couldn't make out anything but blurry shapes. He blinked and tried to turn over. Pain shot through his arm. He gasped and immediately stopped moving. He tried to lift his arm to shield his eyes from the light, but somehow he couldn't get it to move.

Disjointed scenes from the night before flashed through his head. He remembered drinking by the river and buying drinks at the bar. The rest of the night hovered just outside his recollection.

Still dazed, he frowned down at his arm. It was taped to a steel rail, and there was a tube stuck in the crook of his elbow.

He jerked against the restraints. "What the hell?" he croaked.

His vision was clearing, and he looked wildly around the room. It wasn't his room or his dad's living room.

It was all white, and he was in a bed with a railing all around the sides. Then he followed the clear tube leading from his arm to a bag hanging on a stand at the head of the bed.

A hospital. He was in a hospital room.

His heart leaped up into his throat. What the hell

happened? Did he get beat up? Wreck his car? What? He squeezed his eyes shut, trying desperately to remember the rest of the night.

Nothing came to him.

Giving up, he looked around the room as far as he could without turning his pounding head, and stared straight into his father's eyes. Even with the edges of the room still kind of hazy, Conner had no trouble seeing the look of total disgust and frustration on his father's face.

"'Bout time you woke up," Mr. McDermott said gruffly.

Conner licked his dry lips and tried to swallow. "What happened?" he asked in a shaky voice.

His father's nostrils flared. He folded his arms on top of his big stomach and turned away from Conner, toward the window across from the bed. "You got wasted and started trouble down at the bar," he said finally. "Bill called me to come get you before they threw you out. When I got there, you passed out cold."

"Man," Conner said. "I'm really sorry."

His father shrugged. "We couldn't wake you up, so I brought you to the ER. Doctor said it's a good thing I did. You were in serious danger of alcohol poisoning."

Conner shook his head. "I've passed out before," he told him. "No big deal."

His father's mouth tightened in disgust, but he

still didn't meet Conner's eye. "You don't get it. Alcohol poisoning is for real. You could have died."

Conner could hear the repulsion in his father's voice. But there was something else, a coldness, a distance, like he was talking to a stranger. *Which he is,* Conner realized. *I'm like some stranger he picked up off the street.*

Conner closed his eyes and turned away from the man next to him. Another wave of nausea rolled through his stomach. He stared at the call buttons next to his hand, concentrating on taking short, shallow breaths until it passed.

Alcohol poisoning.

Could have died.

Then it hit him. *Really* hit him. His mother, Elizabeth, Tia—they'd said he had a problem. He closed his eyes, hearing his mother's voice in his head. How the alcohol was in control, not him. His cheeks burned with shame. All that time he'd thought his mother was just weak. He was bigger than that, bigger than a stupid drink.

Except he really wasn't. Not at all.

Elizabeth Wakefield

As I was getting dressed today, I realized that I used to spend so much time every morning figuring out what I could wear that Conner would like. All I wanted was to make him happy and to make him want me. It wasn't even just my clothes—it was everything I did.

And now, after all the stuff we've been through, I can't imagine feeling that way again. Yeah, it's silly to care so much about a guy that you let yourself get obsessed like that, making your world revolve around him. But it's also kind of simple in a way. You have a goal to work toward. You know what you want, and all you have to do is try and get it.

But I don't know what I want anymore. I'm past that point of rearranging my life around his. I can't do it if he's going to keep scaring me like this, pushing me away and running off without an explanation. I could forgive him for cheating on me with Tia, even though that hurt like crazy. But I still loved him then. I wasn't afraid of him.

I know he's in trouble and his life is unraveling, but I don't know how to fix it. Besides, is that really my job?

I guess this whole thing comes down to one question—

Does it make you a terrible person if you just reach your limit?

CHAPTER
On the Way Back
4

Andy shuffled toward the exit of the auditorium after the college-prep lecture wrapped up, filing behind the rest of his classmates. His head throbbed, and his stomach was twisted into a million knots.

His future was beyond blown. He was going to be stuck in Sweet Valley forever.

Mr. Nelson had been absolutely right. Andy should have started preparing for college months ago. His resolutions to ace all his classes, gather college applications, and rack up a stunning list of extracurricular activities had lasted all of a week. *Almost.*

But it wasn't like he hadn't had other things on his mind. Little things like whether or not he was actually gay and how to tell his parents.

Still, he should have done something about this college stuff. Now it was probably too late. He'd be stuck in some small, local school while his friends went off to live the party life in fun college towns.

Andy shoved his hands into the pockets of his baggy jeans. He took a deep breath and continued moving down the sloping aisle to the exit.

The two biggest brainiacs in his calculus class walked along in front of him, waiting to squeeze through the double doors into the hallway. The taller, rounder one, Jeffrey Burner, pushed his glasses back up on his nose and smiled at Andy. "Hi, Andy."

"Hey," Andy responded listlessly.

Jeffrey's friend, Neil Davis, looked paler than usual, which Andy didn't think was even possible. "I'm shooting for Harvard or Yale," Neil said to Jeffrey, "but I'm applying to Berkeley as my safety school."

Jeffrey frowned. "Cal Poly and Georgia Tech are my safeties," he said.

Andy rolled his eyes.

"I'm pretty worried about that A-minus I got in trig last semester, though," Jeffrey continued.

Neil shook his head. "That was tough," he said sympathetically. "But I'm sure one A-minus could be overlooked."

Jeffrey shrugged, his shoulders sagging slightly. "We *are* competing against the most talented students in the nation," he reminded Neil.

Andy blinked. Were these guys for real? They made an A-minus sound like a complete tragedy. Andy was glad Jeffrey hadn't seen his grades. He'd probably break into tears.

Jeffrey turned to Andy. "So where are you applying?"

Andy flashed on the guide to colleges he'd thrown under his bed a couple of weeks back. After reading pages of entrance requirements, it had been painfully obvious he'd be lucky to get into Bob's U Drive 'Em Trucking School. He tugged at his short, red curls. "Um, I haven't really decided," he said lamely.

Jeffrey nodded. "So many choices, huh?"

"You have no idea."

They had made it through the doorway and out into the hall. Jeffrey and Neil pushed their way through the huddle of people toward the appointment list taped to the puke green wall. Andy hung back, waiting for the crowd to clear a little before he wormed his way close enough to read the list. He squinted at the tiny print, trying to follow his name across the line.

Marsden, A. Wednesday, 11:15 A.M.

The knot in his stomach tightened. *Great.* Two whole days to decide what to do with the next four years of his life.

"Hey, Liz! There you are."

Elizabeth's breath caught, and she cringed into her locker. She knew that voice, and the sound of it made her heart rate speed up. Not in a good way, though. Not this time.

She had no excuse for avoiding Evan's calls yesterday, which was why she'd managed not to run into him at all today. Until now. Five more minutes and she would have been out of here too.

Clutching her French book in her fingers, she peered around the open door of her locker. Evan was leaning up against the locker next to hers. "So where've you been all day?" he asked as soon as he saw her face.

Wherever you weren't. She cleared her throat. "Just classes," she answered. "Oh, and I had an *Oracle* meeting at lunch." Which she hadn't, but the *Oracle* room had seemed like a good place to hide out.

Evan kept his gaze focused on her intently. "I called a couple of times yesterday. Did you get my messages?"

"Oh, I did, um, yeah," she stumbled. "Sorry about that. It's just I had so much stuff to do that I didn't even have a second to stop, and by the time I did, it was after ten, and I figured it was probably too late," she overexplained. But autopilot had kicked in, and she couldn't slow down. "I mean, is ten too late? You know, just so that I know for next time."

"Don't worry about it," Evan said, frowning slightly. His long, black hair hung over his face, half hiding it.

"I really did want to get back to you," she insisted, even though he'd accepted her story. "I didn't know what to—"

He held up a hand, cutting her off. "Hey, you needed some space. It's not a problem. Things have been pretty weird since Conner bailed. You don't have to explain."

She smiled at him, grateful that he was making this so easy. What had she been so afraid of anyway? How had she managed to forget that with Evan, things were always simple? He wasn't complicated like . . . some people.

"Thanks," she said, easing her French book back into her locker.

"You're welcome." He tilted his head to the side, letting the hair move away from his face, and returned her smile. His dark blue eyes got that gleam she'd started to look forward to seeing, and she let her gaze linger on them a little, a tingly sensation rushing through her.

This is wrong. She had no place looking at him like that. Tia and Jessica would be all over her. And she really shouldn't be feeling what she was at this second.

But she did feel it. And there was no way to hide it from herself anymore.

Evan brushed back the flannel shirt he wore open over a plain white T-shirt, resting his hand on the side of his waist. "So how are you?" he asked. "Any news on the Conner front?"

Elizabeth's smile faded. She turned back to her locker, rummaging around as if she were still looking for something in there. "No, nothing new to report," she answered lightly. She yanked the French book back out, holding it in her hands without having a clue what to do next.

Evan laughed as he gently plucked the book away from her. "Are you sure?" he prodded. "Because you just put this away."

His arm brushed against hers as he moved forward to put the book back into her locker. The touch sent a shiver skittering down her spine. Which meant nothing. Nothing.

She sighed, stepping back from her locker. "Okay, I'm not all right," she admitted.

He stared at her encouragingly, waiting for her to continue without pushing her. The way he always did.

Elizabeth licked her lips, trying to regain control of her body. But Evan was standing there in front of her, so warm and supportive, so strong. How was she supposed to resist letting him be there for her? Letting her comfort her and maybe . . . more.

Because it's disloyal to Conner. And Jessica.

Not to mention Tia, who'd go crazy if she walked down the hallway and spotted them standing so close to each other. It wouldn't be hard to pick up on all the tension between them right now. Even Elizabeth wasn't able to deny it any longer. But still, why did everyone expect her to go through this all alone? Why wasn't she allowed to have help? To need someone?

"I am worried about Conner," she admitted. "I

really am, but—" She stopped, suddenly realizing that if she told him how she really felt, Evan would finally see that she was a selfish, bad person.

He leaned forward. "But?"

She played with the lock on her locker, spinning it around.

"You don't have to tell me if you don't want to," Evan added. "But I have a feeling I'll get it out of you somehow."

"Oh, really?" Elizabeth said, cracking a smile. Evan could be pretty arrogant—but in such a sweet way.

Evan scratched his head like a cartoon character would. "Let's see, well, there's always torture."

She managed a laugh. "I thought you were a pacifist."

"I could bend that rule under extreme circumstances," he answered. "But it would probably scar me for life. So you'd better just tell me."

The truth was, if anyone out there wouldn't judge her for what she'd been thinking, it was Evan. And he was right—she'd end up telling him the truth sometime, so why not get it over with?

"I'm just getting so tired of all this," she blurted out. "Yes, I care about Conner, but I can't drive myself crazy worrying about him anymore. I mean, when is it going to end? I'm sure Conner will come back eventually. But what then? What if he just keeps drinking and going off on everyone?" She stopped and stared down at the floor. "I know I'm being self-ish," she whispered, "but I'm not really sure how much more of this I can handle."

"Hey." Evan touched a finger to her chin and gently lifted her head upward so that their eyes met. "You're not selfish," he said. "We've been over this."

Elizabeth tried to look at him, but the intensity in his eyes was too much. She jerked her gaze back down to the scuffed-up linoleum.

"Well, if you're so convinced that you're selfish, then I guess that must mean I'm selfish too," Evan went on. "I'd like to give him a serious kick in the butt for putting everybody through this."

Elizabeth slowly raised her eyes to meet Evan's again. "Really?" she said, swallowing hard.

He nodded. "Definitely."

It amazed her how he always seemed to know how to make things okay, or at least more okay than they were five minutes ago. "It's just . . ." She trailed off, letting out a deep sigh. "Sometimes I just want to be a regular high-school senior, you know? Doing—I don't know—normal high-school kind of stuff."

"High school, huh?" Evan said. "Personally, I'd prefer to be doing whatever you do at a *beach resort*. But that's cool. Beach resort, high school—we all have our dreams."

Elizabeth laughed, punching him lightly on the arm. His very toned, lean swimmer's arm. Ugh—why was she *noticing* that?

"Yo, Evan," a voice called out behind them. Elizabeth jumped, instinctively stepping back from Evan. She turned and saw Dave Cantrell, another guy from the swim team, heading toward them. Her whole body relaxed as she realized it wasn't one of their friends. Dave raised a hand in greeting. "You'd better get going," he told Evan. "We've gotta be in the pool in five."

Evan nodded. "I'll catch up with you," he said as Dave passed them. He pushed himself away from the lockers. "I do have to go," he told her. He paused. "Why don't you come to the meet?" he suggested. "It'll only last an hour. We could get something to eat afterward."

"I can't," she said automatically. "I've got math and English, and—"

Evan shook his head. "And you need a break." He gave her another tingle-inducing grin. "I'm going for a record in the two-hundred-meter freestyle today. I swim way better with a cheering section." He winked. Actually winked. "You wouldn't want to be responsible for me losing out on a record, would you?"

Elizabeth laughed. "Evan, I believe what you're doing is commonly referred to as emotional black-mail."

"Could be," he admitted.

She grinned up at him. The guy *was* certainly persuasive. And he was making her laugh—something she needed right now more than anything else. She shoved her books back into her locker and slammed the door. "Okay, okay. I'll go."

Jessica pulled her SVH shirt over her head and grabbed her practice shorts. She wanted to get out onto the field in time to warm up before Coach Laufeld started drills.

"Hey, Jess, do you have a sec?" Tia asked, dropping down on the bench next to Jessica. She pulled her long, dark hair back into a ponytail, wrapping a green scrunchie around it.

"Sure," Jessica said. She stood up and pulled on her shorts, then sat back down to lace up her sneakers.

"I just wanted to let you know that I'm dropping out of the dance committee," Tia mumbled.

"What?" Jessica let go of her shoelaces and glanced up, fixing Tia with a hard glare. She was not going to let someone else drop out on her.

"Look, that whole college-admissions assembly really scared me. I just need to spend more time on my schoolwork. So . . . sorry," Tia said, continuing to fidget with her ponytail even though every hair had been smoothed into place.

"What are you talking about?" Jessica demanded. "Your grades are fine." She couldn't believe this. She'd gotten her friends together on this homecoming-dance committee so they could all forget the sucky stuff going on in their personal lives and make their last dance together really great. Now, one by one, every single person was giving her a new excuse. "Tee, what's really going on?" she pressed.

Tia stood up and started stretching, still avoiding Jessica's gaze. "Okay, so it's not for me," she admitted. "I sort of promised Andy I'd do whatever I could to help him raise his grade-point average, and he asked me to help him that night."

Jessica let out a choked laugh. "Okay, Tia, now I *know* you're bluffing. Andy Marsden does not do schoolwork, especially when he could be partying instead."

"Which is exactly why he needs my help so badly," Tia argued.

"Tia, I'm not buying it," Jessica persisted. "That is not a good reason to quit on me. Now, tell me why you're doing this, for real."

Tia sank down on the bench next to her, running her hands along her shorts. "All right, I'll tell you, but you're not going to like it," she said. "It's just that I had a big blowout fight with your sister Saturday, and I really don't want to have to face her anytime soon."

Jessica slowly let out her breath. So that was it. Score another one for Elizabeth. The girl was doing a great job of messing up Jessica's life lately.

"If that's it, then there's no problem," Jessica said.

"She already quit the committee, so you won't have to deal with her at all."

"Really?" Finally Tia met Jessica's gaze, her own large, dark eyes filled with confusion. "Why?"

Jessica shrugged. "Let's just say you're not the only one having trouble dealing with the way my sister's acting lately," she said.

"Wow," Tia replied.

"Yeah." Even though she knew Tia was on her side with this one, Jessica wasn't really in the mood to rehash the topic. "So anyway, the point is that you can stay on the committee," she said quickly.

"She'll still be at the dance," Tia pointed out.

Jessica shrugged. "Probably, but so will the *entire* rest of the school. It's not like anyone is going to force you to talk to her. Come on—you're the captain of the squad, remember? You really can't miss this."

"I guess you're right," Tia said slowly. "If I don't have to be around Liz, I don't mind being on the committee. But I really did have plans with Andy for Friday, so I'd have to break them. And after the way I've treated him lately, that's not a great idea."

"We'll convince him to come to the dance," Jessica promised. "Don't worry—I'm sure we can talk him into it." Jessica finished tying her shoelaces, then got up and grabbed a ponytail holder out of her locker to pull her own hair back into a ponytail.

One disaster averted. Not bad. Although it wasn't like she didn't still have things to deal with.

Like finding a date for the dance.

She'd been trying not to worry about the fact that she didn't have one, telling herself she'd think of someone before it was too late. She'd even been considering asking Evan since they were pretty good friends now. No potential weirdness factor or mixed messages. But now he was Elizabeth's . . . *now he was Elizabeth's what?* Her sister had sworn up and down that they were "just friends" and that "nothing" was going on between them.

Well, then, I should probably take her word for it, shouldn't I? She pulled her ponytail extra tight and jogged out of the locker room toward the practice field. If all else failed, she could still give Evan a call.

Pepperoni pizza and salad. No, Melissa decided, she wanted tacos and a humongous Coke. Or maybe tacos *and* pizza.

She let out a deep sigh as she watched Coach Laufeld stride off toward the gym. Practice was over, finally. She was sore, tired, and hungry. And completely sick of working on special cheers for homecoming.

It would be different if Will were playing. So different. Everything would be like it should have been—him playing the star role on the field, her grabbing the crowd's attention and firing them up.

Only now she couldn't care less if Sweet Valley even won.

Melissa straightened her legs out in front of her and bent forward, reaching for her toes. The stretch felt great on the backs of her stiff calves. She let her head stay bent over her body, her arms reaching forward.

Jessica Wakefield and Tia Ramirez were a few feet away, and she was in no hurry to sit back up and come face-to-face with Jessica again. She could only imagine how triumphant the little witch must be right now. Raising her head slightly, she risked a peek at the two of them. Tia was standing up, but Jessica still sat cross-legged on the grass. As Tia started to walk away, Jessica looked up at her, one hand shielding her eyes from the late afternoon sun. "Thanks for not bailing on the dance committee," she said.

Melissa stayed perfectly still, pretending to keep stretching while she listened.

Tia shrugged. "No problem. Just make sure your sister stays far away from the whole thing. I am not even close to wanting to speak to her yet."

Jessica groaned. "Believe me—I feel the same way," she said.

Melissa smiled. At least things weren't perfect for Little Miss Jessica either. She sat up, slowly dragging her tired legs together. Behind her, she heard giggles from another group of cheerleaders and turned to see what was going on.

"Can you believe it?" Annie Whitman screeched. "I heard they're getting this band that played on *Talent Search.*"

"That's so cool," Renee Talbot replied. "I hope Brad asks me to go," she said in a stupid, dreamy voice.

Annie caught Melissa looking at them and grinned at her. "Aren't you so excited about the dance?" she asked. "I mean, Will can come on his crutches, right?"

Yeah, he could, she thought. If they only knew . . .

Before anybody else could open her mouth, Melissa grabbed her backpack, jumped to her feet, and took off across the field toward the parking lot. She was out of here. Her school clothes could stay in her gym locker. It wasn't worth spending even one more second around these airheads. If she heard anyone else babble about homecoming dances or football, she was going to puke.

When she reached her car, she had the door open before she noticed that Ken Matthews was unlocking his Trooper a couple of cars away. A blush crept over her cheeks as she remembered the last time they'd talked. It had gotten a little more intense than she'd planned—she'd ended up crying all over the guy. Pretty embarrassing. She considered ducking him, but it was too late. The moment Melissa turned her head to get into her car, she heard his deep voice calling after her. "Hey, Melissa."

"Hey," she answered, her voice flat.

He tossed his gym bag into the front seat and came around his car toward her. "Long practice?" he asked.

Melissa groaned. "Too long," she said, running her fingers quickly through her hair. She couldn't help wishing she hadn't run into him looking like a sweaty mess. Ken always seemed to see her at her worst. Not that she should care how he saw her, really. She barely knew the guy. Maybe that was the problem.

"Yeah, ours was pretty grueling too," Ken said. He leaned back against the side of the white Jeep parked next to Melissa's car. "Don't tell anybody, but I'll actually be glad when homecoming's over."

"Me too," she answered automatically, without even making an effort to hide her true feelings. But she had no idea why Ken would say that. She was dreading the whole thing—from *trying* to make it through the night without Will to *trying* to act like everything was normal. But Ken was the big man around campus lately. Why wouldn't he be looking forward to the dance?

Ken cleared his throat. "I was just wondering," he said softly. "Is Will coming to the dance?"

Melissa stared out over the tops of the other cars. "Not unless they're planning on moving it to his house," she said bitterly. It was pointless pretending to Ken that things weren't bad—she'd already made the truth clear when she broke down in front of him.

"So . . . I guess you don't have a date."

Melissa jerked back her head, staring up at Ken in surprise. "No, I don't," she admitted.

Ken nodded, shoving his hands into the front pockets of his cargo pants. "Yeah, me neither."

Melissa gave a short laugh. "That's great. The star quarterback and cheerleader are going alone, huh?"

"Doesn't look too good, does it?" Ken asked, shaking his head.

"There's no reason Will couldn't go," Melissa added, resentment building up inside her. Yeah, he wouldn't be up to dancing. But he could show his face, be there for *her*. She didn't need to dance anyway.

"Maybe he's just not up to it yet," Ken offered. "It's too bad 'cause all the guys would really like to see him." He paused. "It must be hard for him, though."

"Yeah, it is," Melissa agreed. "But he's not doing anything about it." She raised her hands and let them drop back to her sides. "I talk to him every day, and—" Her voice cracked. "He still won't let me see him," she finished quietly. "He won't talk about coming back to school. It's like he's just going to sit in that room and rot away or something. And there's nothing I can *do* to stop it."

"That sucks," Ken said, staring at her with genuine sympathy in his light blue eyes. "I know he's in a rough spot, but none of this is fair to you either."

How sad that Ken could get that when Will, her own boyfriend, was still clueless.

"No, it's not," she agreed. She shifted from one foot to the other, giving her head a light shake. "You know, we planned to go to college together and everything. But now that his scholarship's blown, I don't even know where to apply, what I should . . ." She stopped, blinking quickly. "My entire life is on hold while he sits there doing *nothing*."

Ken pursed his lips, still watching her closely. "Well, you have to start figuring things out for yourself, I guess," he said. "Without him."

Melissa gave a shaky laugh. "Right. *That's* easy." She could barely remember what it was like to imagine a future that didn't involve Will. Even when he broke up with her for Jessica Wakefield, she knew he'd come back to her eventually. And he did. She was sure then that nothing else could stand in their way.

"You're a good student, right?" Ken continued. "You could probably get into a lot of places. You've tried to be there for him, but he's not letting you. And—well, sometimes you think someone really cares about what's right for you, but it turns out they don't and it's up to you to go for it on your own."

She had a feeling from the suddenly sharp tone of his voice that he was talking about himself, not her. She'd heard he split with Jessica's friend Maria. So he really did know how she felt right now.

She smiled up at him, grateful to hear exactly what she'd already been telling herself. She hardly knew Ken, but he always seemed to say the right thing.

And do the right thing. He'd gone all the way from quitting the football team back to being the star quarterback. Melissa straightened up and eyed the football jersey pulled tight across his muscular chest.

Ken Matthews was on his way back.

And so am I.

To: marsden1@swiftnet.com
From: 6hanson@cal.rr.com
Time: 3:25 P.M.
Subject: Just checking in

Hi, Andy:
   I haven't had a chance to talk to
you at school lately, and I've been
really wondering—how did it go,
talking to your parents? I've seen you
in the hall, so I know they didn't
kill you. . . .
   Send details.
                              Six

To: 6hanson@cal.rr.com
From: marsden1@swiftnet.com
Time: 4:39 P.M.
Subject: re: Just checking in

Six—

No, I'm not dead. But my parents
are sending me to New York next week
for years of intensive psychoanalysis.
If that fails, I'm going to study
fashion design.

No, just kidding.

Mom and Dad were great. Wonderful.
Perfect, even.

You were right. I needed to tell
them.

Thanks for asking. I mean it.

Andy

CHAPTER

5 Major Meltdown

Conner glared at the wheelchair, bile rising in his throat. "I really don't need that. I can walk just fine."

The small, gray-haired nurse's assistant smiled patiently. Her tiny, age-spotted hands tightened on the handles of the wheelchair blocking the doorway to his room. "Hospital procedure, honey," she said firmly.

"Great," Conner muttered. He sighed in frustration, then sat gingerly in the wheelchair. He was twice the woman's size. He felt like a total idiot.

Not like *that* was anything new.

He expected her to have to grunt and strain to pull him around in the chair, but surprisingly the wheels moved easily as she pushed him briskly down the hall to the elevators.

The elevator was huge inside. Big enough to hold gurneys, he realized.

Like the one I came in on . . .

The idea blew his mind. He couldn't picture it. Had he been awake? Talking? He shuddered. He still couldn't remember a thing after his father showed up at the bar. Talk about a major meltdown.

Riding down in that huge elevator, one thought wouldn't go away. He could have died. *Died, as in dead. Gone.*

Conner tried to swallow, but his throat was completely dry. He closed his eyes and let the woman push him out the front doors. Once they were at the curb, he moved to get up.

The aide put a hand on his shoulder. "Let's wait until your father gets here, dear."

Conner sank back against the vinyl backrest. He twisted the white plastic admittance bracelet around on his wrist, carefully avoiding looking at the gauze still taped to the crook of his elbow where they'd stuck the IV.

His father's dinged-up old Ford Ranger pulled to a stop right in front of him. Mr. McDermott stayed put in the driver's seat and stared straight ahead, so all Conner could see was his profile and the tight set of his mouth as he waited for Conner to get in.

The aide patted him gently on the shoulder. "You take care, sweetie," she said softly.

Conner nodded. "Thanks," he muttered, then jumped in the car.

Great. Everybody in the whole damn hospital probably knew what a total loser he was.

His father pulled away from the curb before Conner even had his seat belt on. Conner leaned back in his seat and closed his eyes. It was going to start any minute. The Lecture.

He knew it by heart. He should—he'd heard it from his mother enough times. *Conner, you don't have control of alcohol. It has control of you. Conner, you don't realize what you're doing to yourself. Conner, you need help. . . .*

But his father drove all the way across town without saying a word. Not one. He turned the corner onto his street, pulled up in front of the house, and turned off the engine.

Conner was wondering how long he was going to get the silent treatment when his father cleared his throat. He stared out the windshield. "I think it's best if you head back to Sweet Valley," he mumbled. His gaze flickered in Conner's direction. "I have other stuff going on . . . other things. . . ." His voice trailed off.

Conner opened his mouth, but nothing came out.

The muscles in the side of his father's jaw tightened. "I wouldn't even know what to do with you. Your mother's the one who would know how to deal with this kind of thing anyway."

What kind of thing? Conner wanted to shout. *A son?* He choked back a bitter laugh. Okay, he got it. He totally got it. The man did not care. Not even slightly.

"That's really great," he said, more to himself than anything else.

He grabbed the door handle and shoved the heavy door wide open. All those years growing up, he'd tried to convince himself that his dad never came around because he was too busy working, running a successful company or jetting all over the world.

Guess again.

The man never came around because he simply didn't care. And if he didn't care then, why would he care now?

Conner headed across the patchy lawn toward his father's house. What kind of man could just erase a child from his life?

Not the kind Conner wanted anything to do with. The realization hit him right in the gut. Michael C. McDermott didn't care. Not about him, not about anybody but himself, obviously. But other people did. People back in Sweet Valley who were probably worried out of their minds.

He closed his eyes tight against the memory of his mother and Megan and Elizabeth and all his other friends crowded together in his living room, trying to get him to see what he was doing to himself.

And he'd blown them off completely.

They'd probably known he was going to do it, but they'd been willing to face him anyway. He winced, realizing how much they had been willing to take from him just because they cared.

He swept into his father's house and headed for the phone in the kitchen. The receiver shook in his hand, and his fingers trembled as he punched in his number.

"Hello?" His mother picked up on the second ring, her voice shaky.

"Mom? It's me." Conner held his breath, waiting for the explosion.

"Conner! Where are you? Are you—"

"I'm fine, Mom," he said quickly.

She sighed into the phone. "Thank God."

He looked around his father's messy house, feeling an overwhelming need to be out of there. "I know I owe you an explanation, Mom, but—"

"Conner, we have to talk. We've got to get you—"

"I know," he cut in a little sharply. He wasn't up to a huge discussion. Not right now. "Listen, I'm okay, and I think I'm ready to come home now." He tried to keep the irritation out of his voice, but he wasn't sure it worked.

She took a deep breath. "You'd better be coming home," she said, "or else I'm going to have to send the police out after you. I promised Megan I'd hold off as long as you came back by today."

"Mom, listen to me," he said carefully. "I'm leaving here in the morning. I'll be back by tomorrow night."

"Conner, I don't want you driving if you're—"

"Mom," he cut in again. "I'll be home tomorrow—

we'll talk when I get there, okay? And I promise, I'll be fine getting home."

"Okay. Because we're all so worried and—"

"Mom, I'll see you tomorrow." He gripped the phone hard. There was one more thing he had to say before he lost his nerve. He had to say it, had to make the commitment, but it was harder to get out the words than he'd expected. "And when I get home"—he took a moment to gather up his courage—"I'm going to check into rehab."

Jeremy uncapped his bright green highlighter, pulled his history book toward him, and flipped to the first page of chapter ten. He would not look at the clock again until he'd finished reading the whole chapter.

Railroads had already transformed life in the East, but at the end of the Civil War the rails still stopped at the Missouri River.

He jammed the cap back on his marker. "And why do I care?" he muttered out loud.

Carefully, not looking at the clock on his night-stand, he stared instead at the white cordless phone a few inches from his fingertips. He tipped back his desk chair, balancing on the back legs, and clasped his hands on top of his head. Jade should have been home from cheerleading an hour ago at least. Maybe he should call her again. He reached for the phone but jerked his hand back immediately. Maybe that would make him look too eager, after he'd already left her a message yesterday.

But he couldn't concentrate on his homework until he talked to her. He groaned. Okay, he'd call, but if she wasn't there, he'd hang up without leaving a message.

Quickly, before he could change his mind again, he grabbed the phone and punched in her number. It rang once, twice, three times. His finger was hovering over the off button when Jade picked up.

"Hello?" she said breathlessly, like she'd been running to catch the phone.

Jeremy leaned forward, surprised to hear her voice. The front legs of his desk chair landed back on the floor with a bang. "Hi," he said, trying to sound casual.

"Hey, there," she said, her tone instantly warmer. "What's going on?"

"Nothing."

Jade laughed, that throaty, teasing laugh of hers. "You called because nothing is going on?"

Jeremy winced. *Smooth, Aames.* He took a deep breath and tried to match her light tone. "I just called to say hi," he explained.

"Well, hi."

He waited, but she didn't say anything else.

"Haven't talked to you in a while," he said finally to fill the silence. *Like since you gave me that really intense card!* his mind screamed.

Jade sighed. He thought he heard fabric rustling, like she was shifting position. "I've been so busy, it's not even funny," she said. "We've got extra cheerleading practices for homecoming, and I swear I've put in ten job applications."

"Wow. Really busy, huh?"

She laughed. "More like frantic. You?"

"Just the usual. Too much homework."

He stared up at the poster of Jerry Rice above his head. How was he going to move the conversation around to what was going on with them? He'd been expecting her to do it. That's how it generally worked, right? The guy talked about nothing, the girl talked about The Relationship.

He should have known it wouldn't work that way with Jade. She didn't do much of anything by the rules.

"I had a good time the other night," Jeremy said, hoping he could steer the conversation around to them.

"Me too," Jade answered. "That restaurant was great. I can't believe Judy Mullen and that dorky boyfriend of hers were there too, though. They are so clingy, it makes me sick. It's like people get into one-on-one relationships and they go brain-dead. Yuck."

"Yeah," Jeremy agreed. Now he was officially confused. Was she saying relationships were a bad thing? Then why had she given him that serious, sincere card?

Quietly, so she wouldn't hear it on her end, he slid open the top drawer of his desk, where he'd stowed The Card.

"Any good gossip at Big Mesa today?" Jade asked.

He pulled out the card and scanned it again. Yep. It still sounded like a girlfriend-to-boyfriend note to him.

Jeremy stared up at Jerry Rice. Did he have these kinds of girl problems? *Doubtful. Very doubtful.*

"Jeremy?" Jade prompted.

"Oh, um, gossip. No, not really."

Jade's line beeped in his ear. "Hang on, I've got another call."

"Sure," Jeremy agreed. He waited while she clicked over the line to answer the other call.

She came back a few seconds later. "It's for my mom," she said. "I'd better go."

"Sure, okay."

"So, I'll talk to you later?"

"Yeah, later," Jeremy said, hanging up with a sigh.

He tapped the short antenna against his closed lips. It was like she'd gone from party girl to girlfriend then back to party girl in nine seconds flat.

Unfortunately for him, he was definitely slower getting up to speed.

"I cannot *believe* I just drank a glass of juiced grass," Elizabeth said, laughing. She leaned her head back against the seat and glanced at Evan across the car. "How did you talk me into that anyway?"

Evan took his eyes off the road for a second to smile at her. "I don't know. Actually, I've never been able to get anybody else to try it."

"Well, it wasn't *that* bad," she admitted. She shuddered, remembering the, well, *grassy* taste. "I don't think I could make it an everyday thing, though."

She studied Evan's profile as he concentrated on driving. This whole afternoon had been really fun, really . . . easy. From watching his swim meet to sharing smoothies at The Garden of Eatin', everything had been so normal, so *high school*. Exactly what she'd told him she needed.

Everything that Conner hadn't been able to offer.

Evan turned the corner onto her street. He glided the car to a stop in front of her house, turning off the engine. "So, feel better now?" he asked.

She grinned. How did he always seem to know just what she was thinking? "Definitely," she answered. "I haven't had such a—" She paused, remembering what Jessica had said. She didn't want to give Evan the wrong impression. "Such a *mellow* afternoon in a long time," she finished.

"It's easy to forget how, huh?"

"It is lately," she agreed.

Evan fixed his gaze on the street outside. "You know," he said, "there's a saying in *The Book of Tao*. Fish should not be taken from deep waters."

Elizabeth pretended to frown thoughtfully. "That reminds me of a saying I know," she said, faking a serious tone. "It goes something like this—guys should not say weird things."

Evan rolled his eyes, but she could see the glint of laughter in them. "Go ahead, make fun," he said, "but one day you'll be begging me for some more of that ol' Tao wisdom."

"Oh, I'm sure," she teased. She glanced down at her lap, tugging down her flowered skirt. She didn't want to get out, but she couldn't think of anything else to say. And images of the last time they'd been here, in his car in front of her house, kept running through her mind. What if he tried to kiss her?

The scary part was—she wasn't sure if she was hoping he wouldn't or hoping he *would*.

Even realizing that the question was there was enough to motivate her to action. "Well, thanks for the liquid lawn," she said, quickly pulling open the passenger-side door. "I, um, really did have a great time. And congratulations on winning the meet."

"Thanks," he said, his blue eyes focused on her intently.

"So, bye," she said, stepping out of the car. She reached down again to smooth out her skirt.

Evan lifted his fingers in a wave. "Bye," he said. "See you tomorrow."

She turned and walked briskly up to her front door, feeling her body relax slightly once she was inside the house with the door firmly shut behind her.

But her muscles tightened up again when she spotted Jessica standing on the bottom step of the stairs, one hand clutching the banister, the other planted on her hip. "Have a nice time with your *boyfriend?*" she asked, her voice dripping sarcasm. She put a hand over her mouth in mock apology. "Oh, excuse me. I meant your boyfriend's *friend.* Sorry." She flounced past Elizabeth and into the kitchen.

Elizabeth watched her sister's rigid back disappear into the other room. Her shoulders slumped. All the positive energy from her light, carefree afternoon drained right out of her, and the stress and guilt slammed into her again.

She stared at the empty living room, wondering if she should go after Jessica. Force her to get past this crazy temper tantrum and accept that Elizabeth and Evan weren't doing anything wrong. Because they weren't, were they?

She sighed, leaning against the cool wall of the foyer. She deserved to forget about Conner for a little while, to forget about alcoholism, and rage, and out-of-control feelings.

She deserved that, and if Evan helped her do it, she had every right to hang out with him. Nobody could tell her differently. Not Tia. And especially not Jessica.

*　　　*　　　*

83

The cabinet was nearly empty. Of course. Her mother was way too busy playing tennis to bother with grocery shopping. Melissa sighed, slamming the oak door shut. She leaned back against the tile counter, surveying the bright kitchen. There was nothing even remotely resembling a bedtime snack here.

She glanced at the digital numbers on the microwave above the stove. Nine o'clock—time to call Will. She grabbed the kitchen phone and punched in his number with one hand while she walked across the kitchen and opened the fridge. She tucked the phone between her ear and her shoulder and bent down to scan the lower shelves.

It took Will the usual five or six rings before he picked up. "Hello?" he said, his tone as flat as ever.

"It's me," Melissa said.

"Hi, Liss."

"Hi." She paused. "So, how's everything?" she forced out in a halfway perky voice.

"The Lakers won."

Melissa rolled her eyes. *Yeah, that's important.* Still, these days anything that got him in anything resembling a good mood worked for her. She spotted a carton of strawberry yogurt behind the celery and snagged it, pulling her head out of the fridge. "Did you get your calculus done?" she asked.

"No," Will answered. "My knee was killing me."

Like every day. She knew he was on a lot of

medicine, and the pain had to be easing up by now. She shoved the refrigerator door shut with her hip. Okay, she'd just ignore his little pity party until he could get over it. "How was home school today?" she asked.

"Didn't have it," he said, sounding happy.

"Why not?" she demanded.

"My knee was really bad, so Mom called and canceled."

Melissa felt the muscles in her neck tense. "Will, you've got to keep your grades up," she pleaded. "You've got to start thinking about—"

"Hey, back off," Will interrupted her. "It's not a big deal."

"Yeah, it is a big deal," she argued. "It's—" *Not worth talking about,* she finished silently. Will cared about the future about as much as the celery in her fridge. "Never mind," she mumbled.

Silence stretched between them. It was pretty pathetic—two people who'd been together as long as she and Will had with nothing to talk about. She pulled the top off the yogurt and grabbed a spoon out of the silverware drawer.

"What are you doing?" Will asked.

She shrugged, swallowing a spoonful of yogurt. "Dinner," she said.

"This late?"

"We had late practice today again." She sighed and rubbed a fist into the tight muscles in the small of her back. "I swear we've got extra practices every minute for homecoming."

"Right. Homecoming," Will responded.

Great. Melissa slammed the yogurt down on the counter. Why had she mentioned the dreaded *h* word?

"This is really great, you know?" Will's voice rose. "This is *my* senior year, *my* senior homecoming. Me, the quarterback. Now I'm missing it all. School, college, everything." He laughed—and the noise came out as a sharp, harsh grating sound. "Senior year, the best time in your life. Right."

Melissa flinched. "Hey, you're gonna graduate," she said. "As long as you keep on top of your work better. And even if we have to start off at a junior college, we can do that. We can—"

"I'm finished," Will practically yelled, as if he hadn't heard a word she'd said. Something heavy crashed to the floor on his end. "Don't you get it? It's over for me. Totally over."

Melissa gripped the phone so hard, her fingers burned. She didn't have a clue what to say. Will was always the stable one, the one who talked her down when she was freaking out. *He* was the one who promised *her* everything was going to work out.

And now he was losing it, and she didn't know how to stop him.

"But Will, you don't have to give up on college," she tried again. "There are lots of—"

"Yeah, right," he jumped in. "Everyone knows what I'm good at. Football. Doesn't do me any good now, does it?"

Melissa closed her eyes. It was like he'd decided to give up on everything the moment his knee had snapped. The phone line hissed impatiently.

"And everybody's going to homecoming," he ranted on. "So I get to sit around here by myself and think about how my future is completely blown while everybody parties and just forgets about me." He let out a ragged breath. "That is so messed up."

"But Will, you could—"

"Could what? Limp out there and watch Ken Matthews take my place? I don't think so." He let out another scary-sounding laugh. "Matthews can't take the pressure, so he quits, then he can't wait to take my place when he doesn't have to fight me for it like a man."

"What does Ken Matthews have to do with *your* future?" she asked, feeling a strange need to defend Ken.

"Oh, nothing, just that he stole it from me."

"Will, Ken didn't *steal* anything," she argued. The guy was going irrational on her. "Ken happens to be a really great guy," she blurted out before thinking.

The phone line crackled in her ear as she waited for Will to respond, realizing what a stupid thing she'd just said.

"That's great," he finally replied, his voice low.

"Now you're standing up for the guy. What, are you going to leave me for him now too?"

"What?" Melissa's mouth dropped as her whole body surged with anger. How dare he treat her like this when all she was doing was trying to *help* him? "You are really pushing it," she said through clenched teeth. "All I'm saying is that whatever Ken does has nothing to do with what happens to *you* now. You and me."

"Yeah, right," Will spat out. "That's why you'll be out there at the game Saturday, cheering on golden boy while I'm lying here in this bed. Thanks for all the *support*, Liss."

She stared at the phone in shock, too furious to think of an answer. He was going too far. Way too far. Without another word, she slammed down the phone, hanging up on him.

It was one thing when Will was throwing his life away and trying to drag her down with him. But now he was blaming her for not *helping* enough? It wasn't her fault if Will planned to lock himself in his house and pity himself to death. And she was *not* going to go along for the ride.

She threw the rest of her uneaten yogurt into the trash can and marched upstairs to her room. The University of Michigan application sat in the center of her desk. Taking a deep breath, she picked it up and opened her desk drawer, shoving it all the way to the back.

Then she pulled out all the other applications she'd stuffed away when she and Will decided on Michigan. She sank down on her desk chair, chewing at the end of a pen. Her appointment with Mr. Nelson was next week. It was time to get it in gear if she wanted to figure out what she was going to do.

Without Will.

Evan Plummer

Reasons to Ask Elizabeth to the Homecoming Dance

1. I need a date.
2. She's not a cheerleader.
3. She believes Tibet should be freed.
4. She actually knows where Tibet is.
5. She could use the distraction.
6. She's smart and funny . . . and gorgeous.
   (Okay, that one counts for ten points.)
7. I know I like her.
8. I think she might like me.

Reasons Not to Ask Elizabeth to the Homecoming Dance

1. Conner McDermott

Senior Poll Category #8
Most Likely to End Up Farthest Away
from Sweet Valley

Jessica Wakefield: Elizabeth Wakefield

Elizabeth Wakefield: Conner McDermott
(He probably already is.)

TIA RAMIREZ: CONNER MCDERMOTT

Andy Marsden: Conner McDermott

Conner McDermott: *absent when ballot was handed out*

Maria Slater: Maria Slater

Jade Wu: Jade Wu

Evan Plummer: Evan Plummer

Melissa Fox: Definitely not Will Simmons

Will Simmons: *absent when ballot was handed out*

CHAPTER

Totally, Completely Numb

6

"Andy, there's been a change of plans," Tia said, standing shoulder to shoulder with Jessica as the two of them faced him down in the empty hallway after school on Tuesday. "You and me," she said, pointing one long, thin finger toward his chest. "Senior homecoming dance. Together."

What? Hadn't they already been through this?

"I think not," he responded, hoping she was joking.

Tia and Jessica exchanged a quick glance and then took another step closer to him, forcing him to back up—straight into his locker door.

"If I were you, I'd listen to her," Jessica said, her expression serious. Her blue-green eyes were narrowed, and her mouth was set in a solid, firm line.

Andy coughed. "Um, I guess I missed something here, but what happened to, 'Hi, my name is Tia, and I think homecoming is stupid. Let's just have a mellow night by ourselves, okay, Andy?'"

"I was confused," Tia replied. "Until Jessica pointed out that it wouldn't look too great for the captain of the cheerleading squad to be a no-show."

"*And* I reminded her how much *fun* it'll be," Jessica chimed in quickly. "Come on, Andy," she pleaded. "You and Tia together—how could that not be fun?"

"Yeah," Tia agreed. "Are you really going to pass up a perfect chance to provide insightful social commentary on the bizarre rituals of our fellow teenagers?"

Andy rolled his eyes. "Pretty weak," he said. "Why is this so important suddenly?"

Jessica's eyes opened a little wider, and he caught a glimpse of genuine emotion. "It's our last homecoming," she said. "Together. I just want it to be great, that's all. And it won't be if we aren't all there."

Andy took in a deep breath, letting it out slowly. He could tell how Jessica had won Tia over—it really was tough to say no to her. Plus it was pretty cool of Tia to suggest they go together. It wasn't like she couldn't find a date if she wanted to. No guy in his right mind was going to turn her down. Well, no straight guy. But she wanted to be there with him. That had to mean something.

"I don't know," Andy joked, cocking his head. "Me with Tia on my arm? How would that look?"

"Smokin'," Jessica teased back, breaking into a wide grin.

Andy nodded. "Yeah, okay. There is that angle." He paused. "Okay, fine, I'll go," he said, flashing Tia a

93

smile. She leaned over and wrapped him up in a quick, tight hug.

"Thanks, Andy," she said, pulling back. "I promise it will be fun."

Andy turned back to Jessica. "What about you?" he asked. "Who's the lucky guy escorting you to this major social function?"

Jessica shifted her gaze away from his, flipping her hair back over her shoulder. "I'm not exactly sure yet," she admitted. Her smile quickly returned. "But don't worry—whoever it is won't possibly be able to overshadow *your* big appearance there."

Andy groaned. That was exactly what he was afraid of.

Conner eased open the front door of his house on Tuesday afternoon. His limbs were stiff from the long drive, and all he wanted to do was flop down on his bed and sleep.

But he had to face his mother first.

He tried to brace himself for the hysterical tears and long lecture he knew were coming. He deserved it—he realized he did now. He deserved that and more. But that didn't mean he felt like dealing with it.

His mother must have heard the door shut because she came rushing out from the kitchen. "Conner?" she called.

He flinched. She rushed toward him, then stopped abruptly a few feet away, as if she were afraid she might frighten him if she came closer. She smoothed down her messy blond hair, taking in a few sharp breaths.

"Thank God you're back," she said, her voice trembling. Her eyes traveled up and down his body, probably searching for everything that was supposed to be there, and he noticed deep worry lines bracketing her mouth.

Conner sighed, trying to figure out what to say next. Slowly his mother came toward him, reaching out to hold him. As her arms closed around him, he stood perfectly still.

"I missed you so much," she mumbled into his shoulder. He let her hug him, not moving away, but didn't return the embrace.

Finally he pulled back slightly. "I—I'm sor—" He stopped, unable to get the word out. "Look, you were right, okay?" he said, turning away from her.

When his mother didn't respond, he glanced back at her. Tears were sliding down her face. He'd dreaded that sight, but somehow it wasn't nearly as bad as he'd expected. The tears he remembered came from drunken, out-of-control sobbing, the loud, sloppy emotions fueled by alcohol. But his mother was sober now.

She calmly wiped away the tears with the side of her hand. "I was hoping you meant what you said last night on the phone."

He nodded.

"Good." She hesitated for a second and then continued. "I hope you don't mind, but after we spoke last night, I went ahead and called my old rehab clinic—"

Conner felt a familiar tightness in his chest. A week ago he would have blown up at her for trying to take control like that, acting like suddenly she had the right to make his decisions when for years she'd left that up to him while she was collapsed drunk somewhere. But the tightness started to ease as he reminded himself that this was what he needed. He knew it, deep down. And he really didn't think he would have been able to arrange it himself.

"No, that's fine," he said.

Some of the tension drained from her face. "Anyway," she continued, "they have a bed available. They can check you in tomorrow."

"Wow. Tomorrow." He had been thinking more along the lines of next week or next month.

Her jaw began to stiffen again, and he knew she was scared he was about to pull out. Was he? *If I don't go now,* he realized, *I probably won't ever go.* She knew that. The clinic knew it.

"Tomorrow works," he said.

Smiling for the first time, his mother squeezed his shoulders, then dropped her hands back to her sides. "I was hoping you'd say that. I'll drive you there in the morning."

He nodded.

"And Conner? I just want you to know, I'm going to do whatever it takes to help you through this." She locked her eyes on his. "Whatever it takes," she repeated.

Conner felt a sharp lump lodge itself in his throat. Swallowing made his eyes sting. He'd been so rough on his mom, so hard on her when she needed him the most, and here she was, sticking by him.

He couldn't help thinking about the stranger who was his biological father. His mom hadn't even asked about him, although he'd told his sister that's where he was. Mrs. Sandborn must have known what he'd find there. His dad had put him up for all of two days and then couldn't shove him out the door fast enough.

Maybe his mom hadn't been parent of the year, but at least she wasn't going anywhere. She was trying. Maybe he could try too.

He wiped his hands along the sides of his jeans, the drops of sweat still clinging to the crevices of his palms. Clearing his throat, he took a step toward his mom, pulling her awkwardly back into a hug. At first she felt stiff in his arms, clearly surprised. Then her arms tightened around him, and she hugged him back.

After a moment he let go, and she gave him a couple of pats on the back, then let her arms return to her sides. "It's going to be all right," she told him. "Really."

"Yeah," he said. "I know." Even though he didn't.

"Can I make you some dinner? Hamburgers?"

Conner shook his head. He had zero appetite. And there was something else he needed to do. "I, um, I have to go see Liz," he said. His tongue felt thick as he said her name. As much as he'd worried about facing his mom, the idea of seeing Elizabeth was ten times as frightening.

"That's a good idea," his mother agreed.

A good idea. Good. Nothing in his life right now seemed to deserve that word. He'd messed up everything so badly. Conner headed for the front door, then stopped halfway out. "Mom?" he called over his shoulder. "Thanks."

He slipped outside and closed the door behind him without turning to see her reaction. Things had gotten as intense in there as he could take right now. He sucked in a lungful of the cool night air, realizing that they were about to get a whole lot more intense.

Elizabeth choked down another mouthful of salad, trying to think of some way to fill the tense silence hanging over the dinner table.

"I found a new online 'zine today," she said in what she hoped passed for a bright, chipper tone. "It's a national news 'zine, and they're looking for teen writers to cover the news from a younger perspective. I'm thinking about applying."

Her father put down his fork. "Honey, don't you

think that might be juggling just a bit much this semester? You've already got the *Oracle* and your job."

Before Elizabeth could respond, Jessica waved a forkful of lasagna in the air. "Don't worry about it, Dad. Liz is great at juggling people—" She stopped to smirk at Elizabeth. "I mean, things."

Elizabeth noticed her parents exchanging a puzzled glance. Why did Jessica have to make such a huge deal out of this? And in front of their parents—it was pretty immature.

She pushed chunks of noodles and sauce around on her plate, wondering how to defend herself against Jessica's nasty comment without giving her parents any hint about what was going on.

Mrs. Wakefield cleared her throat. "Jessica," she began. "Will you have practice late again tomorrow?"

Jessica nodded, her mouth full. "Uh-huh," she answered after she swallowed. "We've got this great halftime routine for homecoming. It's—"

The chime of the doorbell rang through the room, cutting her off.

Elizabeth glanced up from her plate, startled. Any interruption was a welcome one at this point.

Mr. Wakefield pushed back his chair. "I'll get it," he said. He stood up and tossed his napkin on the table. An instant later he was back.

"Liz, it's Conner," he said, gazing at her with tight lips.

"What?" Elizabeth blurted out, nearly knocking

over her water. Her dad had it wrong somehow. There was no way that . . .

Conner's here? Too many thoughts, too many emotions crowded into her brain for her to make sense of them. Why now? What did he want? Was he out there waiting to scream at her again or to apologize? She seriously doubted the second possibility was true, but still—at least he was safe. Underneath all her confusion, she was aware of a deep relief just to know Conner was okay.

"Um, all right," she finally said. Her knees trembled as she got up from her chair, being careful not to meet Jessica's gaze. She could still feel her sister's glare without even looking in her direction.

"Wait—Elizabeth," her dad said, before she could make her way out of the room.

"Yes?" she said, trying to keep her voice steady.

"I don't want you getting into a car with that boy," he said.

Elizabeth gulped. "No, of course not," she said. She never would have considered it anyway. She was amazed her dad had even let Conner in the house after everything she'd told her parents about the past couple of weeks.

"Okay," she said under her breath, more to herself than the rest of her family. Then she turned and headed out into the living room.

As soon as she reached the doorway, she saw him. He stood in front of the sofa, his hands stuffed in the pockets of his rumpled jeans. His head was sort of tucked down between his hunched shoulders, and he was rocking back and forth from one foot to the other, as if he had no idea where to even stand.

Elizabeth hesitated in the doorway, equally unsure what to do with *her* body. It was Conner, obviously. She had every detail of him memorized—from the way his short, spiky dark hair felt against her fingers to the exact slope of his shoulders. But still, something about him seemed completely different.

Or maybe it's just how I feel, seeing him, she realized with a strange sensation in her stomach. The tingle of excitement that used to run through her every time she caught sight of him wasn't there. Instead she was just . . . sad. Sad and even a little afraid.

She forced her shaking legs to move across the room, stopping when she was within a few feet of him.

"Hi," she said softly. She clasped her hands in front of her body, as if they could act as some sort of barrier between them.

"Hey," he said.

Now that she was closer, she noticed how red his eyes were and that he had deep bags underneath them. She lifted her gaze to a spot just beyond his left shoulder, unable to look directly at him.

Conner tapped the heel of one foot against the toe of his other shoe. "I'm sorry I showed up like this," he said, "but I just got back, and I thought we should talk before I—I just thought we should talk."

She nodded. "Yeah, I guess so," she said.

They were both silent, and Elizabeth glanced down at the carpet, the veins in her head throbbing. Then out of the corner of her eye she saw him move toward her, his arms stretched out awkwardly to hold her. She flinched, instinctively taking a step backward.

Conner's head snapped back. Disbelief, then hurt flickered across his face, before being replaced by the usual blankness that signified he was shutting down—putting up the wall.

"I'm sorry," she mumbled, pressing her lips together.

He shoved his hands back into his pockets and let out a deep sigh. "No, it's fine," he said gruffly. "Whatever. Look, I just wanted you to know that— I'm sorry. I was a jerk, okay? I know it."

Elizabeth nodded again, still unwilling to meet his eyes. Why hadn't she been able to let him touch her? Hugging Conner used to be something she fantasized about every second of the day, and lately she'd longed for it even more—for any reassurance that he still cared about her. But maybe she'd lost sight of her *own* feelings somehow.

"You guys were right," he continued, the words getting harder to hear as he lowered his voice and directed it at the floor. "I, um . . . I need help." He stopped, probably waiting for her reaction. And she should have one, she knew. He was saying everything she'd wanted to hear. Everything that should be making her ecstatically happy. But instead there was just this *emptiness* where the feeling should be inside her. In an abstract way, of course she was glad he was getting help. She was more than glad. But it was as if while he'd been gone, she'd turned off some switch that allowed his words and actions to have such a huge impact on her.

"Well, anyway," he went on when she didn't say anything. "I'm going into rehab tomorrow. I figured I'd let you know."

She forced herself to meet his gaze, finally feeling a twinge of real emotion as she stared into his bright green eyes. "That's great," she said. "That you're going to a program. I'm really happy for you."

"Thanks."

It was like a conversation between two people who barely knew each other, not a couple who just weeks ago had been so close. Scenes rolled through her mind as she stood there, her body tight with nerves. Conner kissing Tia. Conner drunk. Conner wild and out of control. Conner yelling at her and trying to throw her out of his house.

I don't want him here.

The thought blindsided her. She winced, over-whelmed with guilt. The guy she loved was dealing with something incredibly major, and she should be

103

supporting him however she could, no matter what he'd put her through. It's not like he'd ever hit her or hurt her in any way—physically.

But she knew, deep down, that something had changed for her. And she couldn't do it—couldn't be there for him anymore. Not if she wanted to come away with anything left of herself.

The brass clock in the center of the mantel ticked off the seconds, and her head pounded even harder.

Conner cleared his throat. "So I was thinking, you know, that it wouldn't be fair for me to expect you to wait around for me," he said. "I mean, maybe it would be better if we took a break for a while."

Elizabeth felt her face pale. So he didn't want her anyway. He'd come here to let her know he was done. *Sorry I treated you like dirt, thanks for everything, and it's over.* How could he?

Anger surged through her, replacing the guilt. What did she have to feel bad about?

"That's a good idea," she managed to say. Her jaw was so tight, she was amazed she could force out the words at all. She was at her breaking point. Beyond it, really.

"Yeah, I thought so," he said lamely. His gaze flicked over her face, but he didn't say anything else.

Deliberately she turned away and let the tense silence hang there between them without making a move to end the conversation. She didn't want him here—but she wasn't going to make this comfortable for him.

"So I'll see you, I guess," Conner said.

Something in his voice made her look back at him, and for a second she remembered everything she used to feel when she was near him. How his shirt smelled when he held her against him. The way her body reacted when he leaned across his car to kiss her that first time. But they were old memories. Not enough to erase everything that had happened since. Not even close.

She took a deep breath. "Yeah, good luck," she said. "Bye."

He smiled—a sad, crooked smile that made her throat ache with tears. "Bye," he echoed, then turned and headed toward the front door.

As soon as he'd left, she sank down onto the couch, feeling everything at once—but also somehow feeling totally, completely numb.

Conner McDermott

It's weird when you use a line that you used to throw around all the time without meaning, except that it's actually true now. Like when you say you're ending things for the girl's own good because she'd be better off or it's what she really wants, and for the first time in your life—you're not lying.

Jessica Wakefield

I <u>hate</u> fighting with Elizabeth. It's the worst feeling in the world.

I remember when we were eight and we fought over whose toy unicorn had the rainbow-colored tail and whose had the curly yellow one. I just knew the rainbow one was mine, but Elizabeth wouldn't listen to me. So I hid it in my sock drawer. She didn't talk to me for two entire days, and I cried myself to sleep until I gave it back.

It turned out later, Aunt Beth <u>had</u> given her the rainbow one.

And then when we were ten, I wanted to have a roller-skating party for our birthday, but Elizabeth wanted to go miniature golfing. She kept trying to convince Mom and Dad that miniature golfing was better, but I just knew skating was much cooler. I told all our friends that Sean Adams, the hottest guy in the fifth grade, was planning on going skating the day of our party. I also told Elizabeth I refused to have a party unless it was at the skating rink. She didn't believe me until I called all my friends and said the party was off.

We ended up going roller-skating. Sean Adams never showed up, and Jamie Willard broke her ankle. Elizabeth didn't talk to me for two whole weeks.

Back then, I always kind of knew deep down that Elizabeth would end up being right. I think that was part of why I got so mad.

But now what she's doing is so _wrong._ How could she string Conner and Evan along like that, especially when she knows I don't want her to go out with Evan?

   I guess what I'm saying is that I may have been wrong about the pony . . . and the roller-skating. And a lot of other stuff. But I'm right about this.

CHAPTER

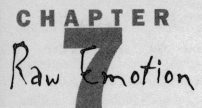

Raw Emotion

Conner pulled his Mustang up in front of the
Ramirez house on Wednesday morning, then let the
engine idle as he drummed his fingers on the steering wheel. He didn't have to see her. He could drive
away right now and go pack for rehab. His mother
or Megan could explain things to his friends.

But Tia deserved better than that. He owed her—
big time.

And finally he was going to treat the people who
mattered the way he should. He stared down at his
white knuckles, remembering how hard it had been
not to get obliterated last night after leaving
Elizabeth. He'd been in so much pain, all he could
think about was the sweet oblivion of being drunk
out of his mind. His whole body had sweated with
the need to get some alcohol in his system. But he
hadn't had a drink. Instead he'd gone home, plugged
in his amplifier, and jammed on his guitar until his
fingers were sore. It almost helped.

And now he had to deal with Tia stone sober too.
He was terrified that she'd be as cold and distant as

Elizabeth or that she'd let loose and go ballistic on him.

Whatever she does, you earned it, he reminded himself.

He turned off the car and climbed out, hustling across the dew-covered grass and stepping up onto the Ramirezes' porch.

"Okay," he muttered to himself. He balled his hand into a fist and knocked hard on the large, white door.

He heard footsteps scurrying around inside, then the blue curtain covering the window beside the door swished aside and Tia's face appeared. Her dark eyes widened in shock. And then she did the one thing Conner had never expected—she smiled.

A second later the dead bolt slid out with a click and the door swung open. "Conner, you're okay," she burst out, her smile broadening.

Before he could say a word, she rushed out onto the porch and wrapped him in a huge hug. When she pulled back and looked up at his face, he saw only relief and warmth in her expression. No judging. No resentment.

"You *are* okay, right?" she demanded, giving him a quick once-over.

Conner stared down at the white porch floor, picturing the room in the hospital he'd ended up in. "Yeah, I'm fine," he told her.

She grabbed the sleeve of his jacket, then tugged

him over to the pine bench near the door and plopped down next to him. "Megan told me you went to see your dad," she said. "What happened? How was he?"

"Hey, slow down." He gave her a small smile, watching as she pulled up the sleeves of her dark blue knit shirt and adjusted herself on the bench so that she could focus her attention on him.

"Okay, I'll shut up," she promised. "Just tell me what's going on."

"Right," he said. "What's going on." He paused. "Um, I'm not really sure where to start." He shifted, blinking when the bright early morning sun hit the right side of his face. He knew he had to get through this for Tia's sake, but he really wasn't up for another big emotional *thing*.

"How about the part where you ran out on a room full of people who were trying to help," Tia suggested, her gaze locked on his.

Conner held his breath. Here it came—the Tia explosion. At least it was a mild dose.

"Okay," he replied. "After I took off, I just started driving. I wanted to get away from everything. I had no clue where I was going." He stopped, remembering all the crazy thoughts and emotions that had been tumbling around in his head. "Then when I got home later, I had this idea about going to see my dad. I needed a way to get away from here, and—I don't know—it just made sense."

"So you found him?" Tia interrupted.

"Yeah."

She raised her eyebrows. "And?"

Conner scowled at the tiny white flowers that bordered the porch. "And he's a jerk."

He heard her take in a sharp breath. "I'm sorry," she said quietly.

"Me too."

Tia sat forward. "Okay, that was a couple of days ago. What happened after that?"

Conner twisted his hands together in his lap. "I don't know. I just was so *sick* of everybody and everything. I wanted to make it all go away." He couldn't look at her, didn't want to see the disgust on her face, so he concentrated on picking at a callus on his palm. "So I drank. A lot, I guess. I, um, ended up in the hospital."

Tia gasped.

"No, it's okay." He stole a glance at her face. She didn't look disgusted at all, just scared. "It's probably a good thing," he admitted. "It wasn't until I woke up in that stupid white bed that I realized you guys were right." He shrugged. "So anyway, I'm going into rehab."

Tia didn't say anything. She just reached out and covered his hand with hers, squeezing hard.

He squeezed back, feeling something lighten inside him. "Before I go," he added, "there's something I have to tell you."

"Okay," she said softly.

He forced himself to turn so that he was facing

her directly. He wasn't wimping out of this. "Tee, I was a real jerk to you," he said. "Some of the stuff I said . . . I just hope you know it's not true." He cringed, hearing the harsh words he'd thrown at her replay in his head. "I know I don't have the best track record with girls," he continued. "But I would never use you. Not on purpose. And I wasn't, I swear."

She nodded, the raw emotion in her eyes cutting through him. He'd hurt her pretty badly, he could tell. But she was still here, ready to accept him. To forgive him. Why? What was so special about him? He was a total screwup.

"So, anyway," he said, straightening up. He moved back to the way he'd been sitting before. "My mom's taking me to the rehab place later this morning. Could you explain things to Andy and Evan and everybody? I know I was pretty crappy to them too, but I can't really deal with all of it right now."

"No problem," she assured him. "Wait—what about Liz?"

Conner's jaw tightened. "I saw her," he said. "She knows."

"And . . . ?" He could see the curiosity in Tia's eyes, but he didn't have the energy to offer any further explanation.

"We broke up," he said. "That's it."

She leaned over and put her arms around him, burying her head against his chest.

"I missed you," she said, her voice low and rough, as if she was on the verge of crying.

Conner squeezed her back. "Thanks," he whispered into her hair.

Gently he pushed her away and stood up. "You'd better get to school," he said. "I'll try to keep in touch while I'm gone."

"Promise?"

There was a word he liked to avoid whenever possible.

"Promise," he agreed.

"I'm not going to lie to you, Andrew." Mr. Nelson leaned across his desk and fixed Andy with a stern gaze.

Lying would be okay, Andy thought. Really, at this point he'd prefer it. Reality sort of sucked. He'd been right to dread his college-planning meeting this morning.

Mr. Nelson took another glance at the Marsden file open beneath his elbows. While he looked, Andy sweated. A lot. Having to see his counselor was worse than sitting in the dentist's office, waiting to hear he had eight cavities. Much worse.

Mr. Nelson shook his head. "Your student profile is pretty thin, Andrew." He leaned forward. "What have you worked on since we last met?"

Andy squirmed uncomfortably on the hard-backed chair facing the desk. He crossed one leg, then the other. "Well, let's see. . . ." He paused, as if sifting through the huge list of accomplishments he had over the past few weeks. "I joined the Outdoors Club," he answered finally.

Mr. Nelson's bushy gray eyebrows raised. "And?"

"And I know all about belaying and rappelling." He fixed Mr. Nelson with a wide-eyed look. "Did you know climbers actually wash their ropes in the washing machine? I had no idea."

Mr. Nelson's thin lips seemed to get even thinner. He flipped back a sheet in Andy's file and studied the page underneath. Then he shook his head again. "Your SAT scores are barely average, your grades are way below what we both know you're capable of. . . ." He sighed. "I'm not sure you realize how difficult it's going to be to get you into the kind of college you'd like to attend, Andrew."

Andy nodded miserably. *No kidding.* He folded his arms across his chest. His stomach was killing him. Was it possible to develop an ulcer in a week?

Mr. Nelson took off his reading glasses and chewed thoughtfully on an earpiece. "I do have one thought," he said after a moment. "There might be room for an admissions committee to consider you if you could demonstrate exactly the sort of work you are capable of when properly motivated." He leaned back in his big, cushy leather chair and crossed his fingers together in front of his face. The reading glasses swung from his hand. "You might be able to spark some interest if you wrote an outstanding admissions essay." He stared hard at Andy, his eyes glinting. "And I do mean outstanding, Andrew."

Andy toyed with the laces on his sneakers. "I guess I could do that," he said. If any of the applications could just come up with a question that actually *meant* something, he'd be okay. Instead of that stupid tell-us-what-matters-most-to-you-in-five-hundred-words-or-less type of thing.

"It's really your best option," Mr. Nelson added. "I hope you take me seriously on this."

Andy felt drops of sweat roll down his back. Sure, that figured. His entire future was going to come down to one gigantic English assignment. No problem.

Is that him?

Elizabeth squinted into the sunlight pouring through the windows at the end of the hallway. The tall shape silhouetted against the light looked vaguely like Evan. Then he turned his back to tack up a piece of paper on the wall, and she saw the battered backpack with the Think Globally, Act Locally sticker plastered to it.

Definitely Evan. Her heartbeat sped up. She'd been dying to talk to him all day.

If she hurried, she could catch him before fourth

period started. She grabbed her creative-writing notebook, slammed her locker shut, and hurried down the hall toward him. "Evan!" she yelled down the half-empty hallway.

He turned, searching the faces in front of him. When he saw Elizabeth, his face broke into a wide grin.

"Hey," he said.

"Hi." She smiled back. "What are those?" she asked, pointing to the sheets of paper in his hand.

"Oh, here," he said, handing her one. "There's an Internet conference next Tuesday on the crisis of nuclear waste in emerging countries. I thought some people might want to check it out."

"Cool," she said. It amazed her how much Evan cared about . . . *everything*. And the way he put so much effort into the things that mattered to him. She was starting to see how lucky she was to be on that list. "Could I talk to you for a second?"

"Sure," he said, resting the tape and posters on a ledge next to him. "What's up?"

She glanced around, wanting to keep this as private as possible. "Conner showed up at my house last night," she admitted.

Evan's expression grew serious. "Really?" he said. He looked away from her, down at the floor, seeming uncomfortable suddenly. She tried not to think about why.

"Yeah, um . . . but it's not what you think," she

said quickly. "Well, first of all, you should know that he's okay." Evan was still Conner's friend—he had been pretty worried about him. "He's actually going to rehab."

"That's great!" Evan said, looking back up at her.

"Yeah, it is." She let her gaze slide away from his. The muscles in her neck and shoulders pulled tight as she imagined the scene with Conner all over again. "But there's more." She ran her fingers along the ledge, playing with the tape dispenser. "We sort of broke up," she said quietly.

Evan didn't say anything, so she figured he was waiting for an explanation. "I don't know; everything just feels all turned around," she said with a sigh. "When I saw him standing there in my living room—I can't even describe how I felt." She tucked a piece of hair back behind her ear. "I know that he's the one who's been through the rough time and that I should just be thinking of him, but somehow I couldn't bring myself to, you know, throw my arms around him and all that. Something was just missing between us."

"So, what did you tell him?" Evan asked. "How did you do it?"

Elizabeth let out a harsh laugh. "Oh, I wasn't even the one who ended it," she said. "*He* broke up with *me*. Something about how unfair it was for me to wait around while he's in rehab." She shook her head. "He wasn't a jerk about it or anything.

He said he was sorry for the way he acted before, but—"

"It still hurts," Evan said, stepping closer.

Biting her lip, she nodded. "But that's not all," she said. "I'm sad about the way things are with us, but in a way, when he told me we should break up, I was almost *relieved*." She glanced up at Evan, searching his expression for a reaction. "Is that terrible? I keep feeling like I'm this horrible person for not being strong enough to be there for him. But I can't, you know? He was right."

"When are you going to give yourself a break?" Evan asked, reaching out to touch her cheek. His fingers lingered on her skin for a second, and she felt herself blush deeply. It was obvious from the way he looked at her how much he cared. "You're an amazing person," he told her, his voice growing strangely thick. "You did everything you could to save him, and something obviously got through because he's getting help."

Elizabeth blinked, realizing that he was right. Conner hadn't gone into any of the specifics of what had happened while he was gone or how he'd figured out that he had a problem. But all that she'd said and done before he left had to have been a part of it, right?

"Thanks," she said, glancing at Evan shyly. "That means a lot."

He smiled. "And besides that, you need to think

of you for a change. I know how you get about the Taoisms, but your first responsibility *is* to yourself."

She nodded without answering. He picked up the flyers again and curled them up into a roll, then smoothed them back out. Roll, smooth. Roll, smooth. The rhythm of his long, tanned fingers had her nearly hypnotized. Then it occurred to her— Evan was fidgeting. Evan. Mr. Mellow.

"Is there something else going on?" she asked.

He opened his mouth, then closed it, dragging a hand through his tangle of dark hair.

"Yeah, actually," he said. "Only my timing really stinks here."

She tilted her head. "What do you mean?"

"Well, I was kind of wondering—are you going to the homecoming dance?"

Elizabeth shrugged. "I hadn't really thought about it." That wasn't exactly true. But ever since she and her sister had gotten into that fight and she'd quit the committee, she hadn't planned on showing up at the dance. Especially since she didn't have a date.

Evan started tapping the roll of papers against his chest. "It's just—remember how you were saying you wished you could just do normal, high-school stuff for a change?" She nodded. "So, I was thinking, maybe you could. Go to the dance, I mean. With me."

Oh.

She knew she should say no. Absolutely, positively no. She'd broken up with her boyfriend, one of

Evan's friends, last night. Tia would have a fit, and Jessica would kill her.

Still, it wasn't like things between her and her twin could get much worse. And Conner *had* been the one to dump her. He was off doing what he needed to do for himself. So why shouldn't she?

"That sounds great," she said, her voice coming out a lot more firm than she felt inside.

Evan's eyes lit up. Actually *lit up*. Conner would never have let himself show emotion like that. It was such a great feeling, knowing she could make Evan happy—and seeing that he wasn't afraid to show her she could.

Conner McDermott

<u>Things to Pack for Rehab</u>

Um . . . I don't actually have to <u>bring</u> anything there, right?

CHAPTER

Something very Close to Hatred

Andy stared down at the limp lettuce on his thin cafeteria hamburger. *Yuck.* He glared at Tia, who was sitting next to him in the half-empty classroom. He could have been scarfing down Mexican food from La Hacienda with Evan and the guys. Instead he'd let her literally drag him into a homecoming-dance-committee meeting.

Lisa Lewis, superperky head of the committee, stood at attention at the front of the classroom. Her shiny blond bob practically quivered with excitement. She clapped. "Good news, people," she said. "We have fifteen dollars left in the decorating fund. I think we should buy corsages for the homecoming king and queen."

People? Andy blinked at her. *People?* Didn't she know that word made her sound like Mr. Nelson?

His hand shot up. He cheerfully ignored the warning glance Jessica threw him from up front and continued waving his hand in the air until he caught Lisa's attention. "Excuse me," he called out.

Lisa's brow wrinkled in surprise. She pointed at him. "Um, yes. You in the back."

Andy sat up and folded his hands together on top of the desk. "Instead of buying a corsage for the homecoming king and queen, why don't we use the money to honor our principal and vice principal, who've been so very good to us over the years?" he suggested in a fake-serious tone.

Tia slunk down in her chair and covered her eyes with her hand.

A hint of panic entered Lisa's eyes, and she glanced around the room as if hoping someone would bail her out. Then she cleared her throat. "I, um, don't really think we need to do that," she finally said. "Any other ideas? Anybody?" she asked, refusing to look in Andy's direction.

He leaned over his desk toward Tia. "You should have known better than to bring me here," he murmured.

Tia winced. "Yeah, fine," she whispered back. "But I had to talk to you. About Conner."

Conner? He'd thought Tia was finally done babbling to him about Conner. Hadn't they been over this?

"He stopped by my house this morning," she explained.

"Oh," Andy said, instantly regretting his reaction. Conner was back in town—that was big.

"He's okay and everything," she said quickly.

"Actually, better than okay. He's checking into a rehab program today. He was on his way there this morning, so he asked me if I'd tell everybody for him."

A mixture of relief and disappointment swirled together in his empty stomach. Conner was his friend, and of course he'd been worried about him. But it still felt like he'd been left out of this whole process somehow. Conner had completely ignored the most major thing that had ever happened to Andy, and now he'd left for rehab without even saying anything to him directly.

"He had to leave right away," Tia added. "He didn't have time to talk to everybody, and he felt really bad about it."

No, Andy thought, *he didn't make time*. But he didn't point that out to Tia. She sounded so happy, truly relaxed for the first time since Conner had taken off. He didn't want to mess that up for her.

"That sounds like our boy," he observed in a light voice. "Wouldn't want to talk any more than he has to."

"True," Tia acknowledged.

"But that's great," he said. "Really great. At least he's doing the right thing."

Tia nodded, and Andy turned back to stare ahead at the front of the room. Lisa Lewis's mouth was moving, but he didn't hear a word.

He kept telling himself that this was good news—

of course it was. But it still stung that he hadn't made the cut for being told personally. If Conner had finally realized that he had a problem and he needed help, hadn't he *also* thought about the way he'd treated his friends lately? How he'd never asked Andy once if he was dealing okay with being gay, coming out to his friends, and whether to tell his parents?

Andy flicked the lettuce off his cold hamburger. Just when he'd thought his friends were starting to come around, he had to get this nice little reminder that Conner couldn't care less about him.

"Okay, the next set of partners will be Elizabeth, and, let's see." Ms. Dalton paused, quickly scanning the room. "Tia," she decided. "The two of you can alternate reading the lines in the next stanza, *s'il vous plaît.*"

Elizabeth's breath caught. How perfect—all she needed right now was to pair up with Tia to read a poem about true love.

She glanced down at her open textbook, trying to locate the poem. *"Quand est-ce que ca le coeur s'ouvre?"* she read out loud.

When does the heart open?

She gulped. In her case, maybe it never had. If she'd really opened herself completely to Conner, would she have been able to close up so easily?

She snuck a look at Tia, who sat two rows over, staring down at the book in front of her.

127

"Le coeur s'ouvre quand l'amour vrai trouve la clef," Tia read in a clear voice.

The heart opens when true love finds the key. Elizabeth translated the line automatically in her head.

She peeked at Tia again. Was she frowning? Yes, she was definitely frowning. Elizabeth's stomach clenched.

"Elizabeth, *s'il vous plaît?*" Ms. Dalton prompted.

"Oh, um, sure." She found her place again and read, *"L'amour vrai naît ne de la douleur—"* The true love born of pain— She stopped in the middle of the line, trying desperately to swallow the lump rising in her throat.

She could feel Tia's eyes on her, and she figured Jessica was probably sending her a matching glare from the other side of the classroom. Only Maria, on her right, wasn't putting out hatred vibes. Then again, Maria was still so depressed over her breakup with Ken that she'd barely noticed what was going on with the rest of her friends. Maybe if she knew, she'd be judging Elizabeth too.

Elizabeth dragged her attention back to the book. *"Le—l'espoir et le courage,"* she stumbled out.

The true love that is born of pain and hope and courage.

Elizabeth stared at the front of the room, tears pressing against the backs of her eyelids. How many times had she cried in the past week? More than in the rest of her life combined? It felt that way. But the words of the poem were hitting her hard. Tia was disgusted with her because she hadn't had the courage to stick it out with Conner. Yeah, he'd broken up with her—but it wasn't like she would have been able to stay with him anyway. She'd known it in her gut even before he showed up at her house last night.

"*Merci,* Elizabeth *et* Tia," Ms. Dalton said. "*Maintenant,* let's have Melissa and . . ."

Elizabeth leaned back in her seat, rubbing her forehead. She risked another glance at Tia, and this time Tia was looking right at her, her eyes narrowed thoughtfully. Elizabeth immediately broke the stare, focusing back down on her desk. She could only imagine what Tia was thinking right now.

She didn't even hear the rest of the poem. All she could do was watch the clock, willing the bell to sound so she could escape—from Tia's glares, from stupid romantic poetry, and maybe, if she was really lucky, from her own overloaded brain, at least for a while.

When the bell finally rang, she jumped up from her seat and started shoving her books into her backpack. But somehow it seemed to take forever, and her fingers kept slipping.

Once she had everything together and the bag zipped up, she stood to leave, noticing that Tia was the only other person left in the room.

I can't do this right now. The thought flashed through her head, and she made her way across the room to the door, her head ducked down.

"Hey, wait," Tia called out. She came up behind Elizabeth, and Elizabeth tensed, waiting for Tia to blast her. But instead Tia put a hand gently on her shoulder. "You don't look too good," she said quietly. "Are you okay?"

Elizabeth stood still, trying to make sense of the situation. Tia was . . . *concerned?* She shook her head. "Not really," she managed to say around the lump in her throat, her voice coming out squeaky.

Tia squeezed her shoulder. "It's okay," she said. "Let's go to the bathroom."

Elizabeth nodded gratefully and followed Tia out of the classroom. She was too exhausted to question her friend's motives. She needed someone, and Tia was here.

Even though the bell had just rung, the girls' bathroom was empty when they got there. Elizabeth leaned back against the wall, wiping at the few tears that had started to spill over. Tia went right to a sink and started running cold water. She dragged a paper towel under the faucet and handed it to Elizabeth. "Here. This will help," she said.

"Thanks." Elizabeth patted her cheeks with the cool towel, figuring the lecture would start any minute now. But Tia just handed Elizabeth a dry paper towel and waited patiently for her to blot the drops of water.

130

Elizabeth drew in a shaky breath. She balled up the towel, tossed it in the trash can, and turned to face Tia, her arms wrapped protectively across her chest. "I thought—I thought you weren't speaking to me," she said, her heart pounding.

Tia shrugged. "I wasn't. But now . . ." Her voice trailed off. "When I saw you with Evan, I kind of freaked," she admitted. "I thought you didn't care at all about Conner." She reached into the pocket of her slim black pants and pulled out a scrunchie. "But I know that's not true. I could tell what it was doing to you, just reading the lines of that poem in class. I love Conner—he's my best friend—but he's put us all through a lot. Especially you." She played with the scrunchie, stretching it between her hands. "If Evan helped, then I'm glad. And I think Conner would be too."

Elizabeth shook her head. "Wow," she whispered. "Okay."

Tia frowned, looking away as she pulled her hair back into a ponytail. "Conner told me that you broke up," she said. "Before he left this morning. He didn't say what happened, and it's none of my business. But I just want you to know that whatever's going on, I'm here for you too, okay?" She cocked her head and glanced back at Elizabeth. "I've missed you, you know."

Elizabeth forced a smile, even though the whole Conner-told-me-that-you-broke-up phrase was doing weird things inside her head. "I've missed you too," she said. And she had. A lot.

"Look, we both care about Conner," Tia said matter-of-factly. "But we also care about each other. So can we just get over all this other stuff? No more bad feelings about me and Conner?"

"And no more bad feelings about *me* and Conner?" Elizabeth said.

"Deal," Tia agreed, sticking out her hand. Elizabeth reached out and grabbed it, laughing. Finally things were starting to make sense again.

Melissa stood in front of her dresser, glaring at the picture of her and Will at El Carro's homecoming dance last year.

No way she was calling him tonight. Not after the way he treated her Monday.

She leaned over the dresser until her nose was only a foot from the photo and studied it. She focused on Will's cocky grin and the way he wrapped his arm protectively around her shoulders, looking straight into the camera, like the whole world was just laid out in front of him.

Back then the two of them had been looking forward to so much. *And he's had to watch it all slip away*, she thought, feeling a twinge of guilt. Yeah, he'd been pretty harsh when they last talked. But being reminded of homecoming must have hit him so hard after how perfect last year's had been. He'd scored a touchdown at the game, and they'd spent the whole night dancing together, perfectly, blissfully happy.

Melissa ran her finger around the edges of the photo, picturing the dance, remembering how the stiff netting underskirt of her strapless blue dress had scratched her waist. And imagining how safe, how amazing it felt to be on Will's arm all night long.

He hadn't been there for her since the accident. But he'd been there for her before. Maybe it was her turn. If she just kept trying, she could get him to *care* again. About her—and about his own life.

She walked back over to her bed and dragged her phone off her nightstand, then sank down on the floor with her back resting against her bed.

"Hello?" his mother answered after only one ring. That was weird. Why was she picking up Will's line?

"Hi, Mrs. Simmons, it's Melissa," she said, frowning. "Is Will around?"

"Um, I'm not sure, dear," Mrs. Simmons replied, sounding very nervous. She put down the phone and Melissa could hear the sound of a muffled conversation. Then the phone was picked up again.

"I'm sorry, Melissa, but he's resting right now," Will's mom said. She was a terrible liar. "Can I have him call you ba—"

"Don't bother," Melissa said, hanging up the phone. *He* didn't want to talk to *her*? After all the effort she'd made to help him, to be there for him? When everyone else had already stopped caring?

She stared down at the phone, feeling something very close to hatred. Will had done some horrible things to her, but she wasn't sure how she'd be able to forgive the way he was acting now.

Suddenly the phone rang, jolting her. What if it was Will? Did he really think he could have his mother *lie* to her and then call her right back like it was nothing? There was no way she was picking up that phone.

It shrilled again, the noise blaring right in her ear.

What if it isn't Will? If it was anyone else, she had to answer. She had to pretend everything was fine unless she wanted to end up as alone and miserable as Will. If he was stupid enough to call back, she could always hang up.

"Hello?" she said cautiously.

"Hi, is Melissa home?"

It was a guy, but definitely not Will. Interesting.

"Yeah, this is Melissa," she said.

"Oh, Melissa. Hi, it's Ken Matthews."

Ken? That was a surprise. But she found herself smiling as she pulled her knees up to her chest.

"Hey," she said. "What's up?"

"Well, I hope you don't think this is out of line," Ken began. "Maybe it is, but I had this idea." He paused, and she leaned forward, intrigued. "I know you said Will wouldn't be up to going to the homecoming dance, but you pretty much have to go, and I really need to be there too."

Melissa laughed. "Really? The star quarterback *has* to go to homecoming?" she teased.

"Yeah, seriously." Ken chuckled. "So," he continued, "I was thinking, maybe you and I could go to the dance together? I figured we both have to go and neither one of us has a date, so I thought . . . you know . . . just a friend thing," he hurried to add.

Melissa smoothed down her purple ribbed tank top, glancing up at the photo of her and Will again. Go to the dance with his rival? That would hurt him—badly.

And like he hadn't just hurt her? Beyond hurt. He'd totally humiliated her when all she was trying to do was reach out to him. Besides, she had no clue when this was going to stop. When he was going to start pulling his life together. And she'd already decided that she wasn't letting herself be pulled down with him.

"I think that's a great idea," she said.

Yeah, she'd go to homecoming with Ken. It was time she stopped worrying about what was good for a guy who clearly didn't care about it himself.

It was time Melissa started worrying about Melissa.

To: trent#1@cal.rr.com
From: jaames@cal.rr.com
Time: 8:52 P.M.
Subject: fwd: Just for kicks

Yo, Trent—
  Heeelp! Relationship advice needed . . .
  I have no clue what's up with this
girl. Remember I told you about that
really intense card she gave me? What
am I supposed to do about this e-mail?
I just don't get what she wants.
  Any ideas? Please???
               —Jeremy the Clueless
>> **To:** jaames@cal.rr.com
>> **From:** jadewu@cal.rr.com
>> **Time:** 4:45 P.M.
>> **Subject:** Just for kicks
>>
>> Hey—
>> It's the SVH homecoming dance this
>> Friday. I have to go. Thought you
>> might like to come too, if nothing's
>> up.
>> Later—
>>   J.

To: jaames@cal.rr.com
From: trent#1@cal.rr.com
Time: 9:16 P.M.
Subject: re: fwd: Just for kicks

Hey, guy—
  What, you think just because I'm a
jock I've got the inside info on
women? Ha. Okay—I'll give this my best
shot. Either she wants you, or she's
just desperate for a date for the
dance. That's my take on this anyway.
Sorry that's all I have for you.
  Either way, I say go for it. What
else are you gonna do Friday night,
pick up an extra shift at HOJ?
                —Trent the Even More Clueless

To: jadewu@cal.rr.com
From: jaames@cal.rr.com
Time: 9:47 P.M.
Subject: re: Just for kicks

Jade—
   I don't have anything going on
Friday night, so sure, I'll go. Sounds
cool.
   Later—
                    Jeremy

Will Simmons

<u>Fun and Exciting Medical Terms</u>

<u>Acute hyperextension:</u> definition: my knee bending backward. Not good.

<u>Anterior cruciate ligament:</u> definition: the thing that snapped in my knee. Not good either.

<u>Arthroplasty:</u> definition: ten-thousand-dollar surgery. Not good, according to my father.

<u>Sutures:</u> definition: the black threads sticking out of my knee. Disgusting.

<u>Restricted motility:</u> definition: Never playing football again. ~~Not good.~~ Life is pointless.

CHAPTER 9

Dropping the Bombshell

Andy flipped on his computer and sat back in his desk chair, watching as the setup images flashed across his screen. He'd promised himself he'd start on his college-admissions essay right after dinner. But maybe he should check his e-mail first. There could be something critically important waiting. *Yeah, like a new forward from my joke list.* It wasn't like he'd lose a lot of time anyway. This way he could *ease* himself into the writing mood.

Andy pushed down on the mouse button, then typed in the information to log on to his e-mail account. Messages scrolled in, one from the Outdoors Club, announcing an upcoming meeting, another from one of his joke lists, and one from—

Conner?

Andy blinked, sitting up. It was dated earlier that morning, way before school started. Since when did Conner get up that early? He clicked on the message, squinting at the screen.

A.—
    Yeah, it's me. Don't faint, okay?

I'm back, but I guess Tia already
told you that. Hey, I'm sorry I
couldn't say this in person, but my
spot in the rehab hospital opened up
right away, and I had to take off.
   I'm sorry. Really. I wanted to say
all this stuff to you face-to-face.
But oh, well. Here goes.

Andy let out a short laugh. Conner, writing
about feelings? This was classic. Then he continued
reading.

I'm sorry I've been too out of
control to deal with what's been going
on with you. I guess I feel like
you're more together than the rest of
us, so you can handle pretty much
anything. But I hope you're doing
okay, and it'll be cool to hang out
with you again when this is all over.
   Take care, man,
   —C.

Andy sat back in his chair and clasped his hands
on top of his head. He stared at Conner's e-mail for a
minute before closing it. So his friend hadn't blown
him off with some lame, secondhand explanation
after all. For Conner, the man of monosyllables, that
note was practically a novel. Andy could only imagine

how much his friend had sweated over it.

Even though he guessed that Conner wouldn't get any e-mail until he got back home, Andy hit the reply button.

```
Conner,
    Good to hear from you, and yes, you
have ticked me off beyond belief. But
when haven't you? (Just kidding.)
    Seriously, everything is cool with
us, okay? Just hang out, do what the
shrinks tell you, and get better.
Speaking of being together, I think
you're about to find out just how
together you really are. I know it
won't be a surprise to me.
    Later,
                              Andy
```

Do it, Elizabeth told herself. *Just walk in and sit down next to her.*

She stood in the doorway to the living room, her back stiff with tension. She'd been standing there for almost a full minute, trying to decide whether or not to walk in the room.

Jessica lay on the floor, propped up on her elbows, coloring in bubble letters that said, Sweet Valley Rocks! with a black pen. The sharp, toxic scent of permanent markers filled the air.

I have to talk to her. It was getting ridiculous—they hadn't done the whole silent-treatment thing in so long. And Jessica could outignore her any day.

Elizabeth forced herself to move forward into the room. "Jess, can I talk to you?" she asked.

Her sister rolled over and frowned at her. Then she shrugged. "Whatever," she said, turning back away.

The squeak of the marker started up again. Elizabeth watched her color for a minute, not sure where to begin. Obviously Jessica wasn't going to make this easy for her. She squatted down next to her, resting on her ankles.

"I think we should talk about this whole thing, you know, Conner, and . . ." Elizabeth trailed off.

". . . and Evan?" Jessica finished for her without glancing up from the poster.

"Yes," Elizabeth said. "And Evan. But can we try not to get so angry at each other this time?"

The marker squeaked loudly. "Okay," Jessica finally said.

Elizabeth sighed, stretching out her legs in front of her. "So, first of all, I thought maybe it would help if I explained to you what was going on with Conner." She reached up to touch the silver chain around her neck, sliding it against her skin. "Because I don't think you really get how bad things were."

She paused, but Jessica didn't look up.

"Jess, do you have any idea how scary it is to be around an alcoholic, especially if you're totally clueless about the whole thing? I mean, I didn't understand why he was acting the way he was, and then when I did, I had no idea how to help."

The marker stopped moving. Jessica capped it and drew herself up until she was sitting cross-legged. She bit her lower lip. "I know how freaked out you were," she admitted.

Elizabeth took the chance to meet her sister's eye, hoping she'd be able to get through to her. "Yeah, I was," she said. "Beyond freaked out. Jess, I was more scared than I think I've ever been in my life. And after the intervention, when Conner took off—I don't know how I would have held it together if it weren't for . . ."

"Evan," Jessica filled in again, her tone much less accusatory this time.

Elizabeth nodded. "He kept reassuring me that none of this was my fault," she explained. "And I needed to hear that."

"But, Liz, of course it wasn't your fault that Conner was drinking," Jessica insisted. She pushed a few strands of blond hair away from her face. "I told you that too."

"But you didn't know Conner the way Evan does," Elizabeth said as gently as she could. She knew her sister didn't enjoy feeling like someone else's advice had mattered more than her own. "Evan helped me see that there was really nothing else I could have done, with Conner being the way he is, even aside from his drinking."

Jessica's expression softened, and she shoved aside her poster and marker. "Okay," she said. "I guess I can see that. I mean, Evan *is* a really good listener." She stopped, her mouth twitching into a small smile. "If he manages to calm *me* down, he's got to be good, right?" she added.

Elizabeth smiled back, relieved. "Right," she agreed. "So . . . are we done fighting?"

Jessica let out a long, melodramatic sigh. "I *guess* so," she teased.

"Good," Elizabeth said. She took a deep breath, deciding that her sister's mood switch made this the perfect time to drop the bombshell. "Because I didn't want to have to avoid you all night at the homecoming dance when I'm with Evan."

Jessica's smile disappeared instantly. "What are you talking about?" she said, an edge back in her voice. "Are you saying you're going to the dance with Evan?"

Elizabeth stiffened. "Yes, I am," she said firmly.

Jessica shook her head. She gathered her poster and marker together and stood up. "You are really unbelievable," she muttered. Then she turned and headed out of the room.

"Wait a second," Elizabeth called after her,

jumping up. "I thought you understood. And anyway, Conner and I broke up the other night. You know that—you heard me tell Mom and Dad."

Jessica spun around, her eyes flashing with anger. "So? You think that's all that matters? Like I'm the dating police or something, and I have to make sure you don't go to the dance with one guy while you still have a boyfriend?" She snorted. "Did you ever think that maybe *I* planned on going to the dance with Evan? You know, me, your sister— the one who's had to watch the love of her life falling all over that slut Jade Wu? Things haven't exactly been easy on me lately either. I've been working really hard to plan this dance, and now I don't even have a date."

Elizabeth reached up to rub her head. She'd had this headache practically all week, and it only seemed to be getting worse. "Jessica, *why* would you be going to the dance with Evan?" she asked, trying to stay calm. "You dated him for about two seconds, and you never even really wanted to be with him anyway. You've admitted that to me plenty of times."

"Evan and I are friends," Jessica replied, her tone icy. "And when *I* say that, I mean it," she added. "But since I don't have a boyfriend right now, I figured I could have fun going with Evan. I was actually going to call him tonight."

"Isn't it a little late notice?" Elizabeth burst out. "Jess, the dance is in two days!"

Jessica didn't answer, but blotches of red appeared on her cheeks. "Just forget it," she finally said. She turned and ran up the stairs. A few seconds later Elizabeth could hear her bedroom door slam.

Elizabeth sank down onto the floor, her head pounding. Why wasn't she allowed to have a life?

I think I'm going to explode, Andy thought, rubbing his overstuffed stomach. But he couldn't help wondering if there was any other reason to go downstairs to the kitchen. Because that would mean heading away from his computer—and from this stupid college-admissions essay.

He'd already made perfectly sugared cinnamon toast, eaten it standing over the sink, then washed the knife, spoon, and plate by hand.

And dried them.

Then he'd wandered back down and microwaved a bowl of popcorn . . . which he'd had to do twice because he somehow burned the first batch. Who knew ten minutes was too long to nuke it?

His mother probably wouldn't appreciate it if he went back and color sorted her Tupperware drawer.

Andy groaned. He blinked a few times and then returned his gaze to the computer screen in front of him. He glanced at the application resting on his desk next to him, even though The Question was already burned into his brain.

What is the most challenging experience you've

faced, and what did you learn from how you chose to deal with it?

His mind was more blank than the empty, glowing word-processing page on the screen, if that was possible.

What about the time he broke ten thousand playing Tetris? That was definitely challenging—it took him at least a few weeks. Or there was also that time when he was seven and all the ants in his brand-new ant farm escaped. Tracking them down with his mom freaking out behind him was big-time hard.

He positioned his fingers over the keyboard and typed . . . nothing. Mr. Nelson's words kept echoing in his head. "And I do mean outstanding."

No pressure there. Not at all.

He could always find another essay on the Internet somewhere. People did it all the time. His finger hovered over the mouse, ready to click on his Web-browser program. But he knew he couldn't do it. With his luck, he'd send in the same essay a hundred other lazy guys like him found. And besides, when it came down to it, he was too much of a goody-goody to pull anything like that anyway.

Okay, no Internet. So he was just going to have to think of something to write about. He let his eyes wander around his room, desperate for anything to spark a thought.

He stared at his closed closet door. Behind it waited a pile of junk from a million failed projects.

Like the blue-and-red mitt from the time his father decided he should play Little League. He was the only kid on the team who never, ever got on base. Not even by accident. Suffering through that season had been challenging.

He sighed. That wasn't going to cut it either. Totally frustrated, he got up, flung himself down on his bed, and stared up at the blank ceiling.

Challenging experience . . .

Challenging experience . . .

Duh. Suddenly he felt like the most supreme idiot on the planet. What had he been dealing with this past month?

Only realizing that he was gay. Only having to struggle with it alone. Only risking complete and utter rejection from everyone he loved when he did decide to share his revelation.

He got up off the bed and sat back in his desk chair, his fingers actually itching to type. He knew exactly what to write.

Andy Marsden

What is the most challenging experience you've faced, and what did you learn from how you chose to deal with it?

The most challenging experience of my life has been figuring out how to deal with who I am. In the world of Andy Marsden, that's not such a simple thing because who I am isn't who everyone else in my life—and the world around me—might want me to be.

At first when I noticed I wasn't thrilled about dating, I thought I just hadn't found the right girl. And then I did meet this really sweet girl, but I always wanted to hang out with her brother instead. I had all kinds of warnings going off in my head, but I ignored them and tried to get closer to my girlfriend. Only every time we kissed, it was wrong. I knew it inside me, and I finally had to listen.

After we broke up, I spent a lot of time lying in bed, just thinking about everything. What did it mean that I felt those things around my girlfriend's brother that everyone told me I should feel around _her?_ Did it mean I was gay? I think I knew the truth, but it was a lot to handle alone. Still, I was too scared at first to go to my friends or my parents. How would they react?

So I held it all inside.

But pretty soon it became too much to keep to myself, and I spilled the truth to my friends. They didn't really say much, and I was kind of annoyed. Couldn't they see what a big deal this was to me? But I started reading stories about teens whose friends said terrible things to them when they came out or rejected them completely. And I realized that the fact that my friends weren't treating me any differently meant that they were there for me no matter what. No matter who I was.

And once I told them that I needed more attention, needed to talk about all this, they came through. The girl I had dated, who is now a good friend, gave me the courage to tell my parents—who have been amazing. They have done everything to convince me that they'll love and support me through anything. One friend, who has been going through his own serious problem, took the time to write me and remind me how much he believes in me.

It's all made me wonder why it was so tough to tell everyone in the first place. My friends and family have been so great. They've helped me see that I don't have to face any challenge by myself, even one as huge as learning to accept a realization like this one. We all have to deal with personal struggles in our own ways, but I've learned that as long as you don't try to do it alone, you've made a good choice.

Jade Wu

<u>Potential</u> <u>Outfits</u> <u>for</u> <u>Homecoming</u> <u>Dance</u>

Crocheted halter top and hip huggers? No—too retro.

Pink silk flowered dress? Big no—too "sweet girlfriend."

Red minidress? Wild, sexy. No—might look "trying too hard."

Black leather jeans and Lycra tank top? Sexy, fun, definitely not an I'm-taken look. Yes!

Jessica Wakefield

Dateless for Homecoming

You heard it here first. I, Jessica Wakefield, have no date for my senior homecoming dance. I guess the one good thing is that I'll never have to experience living through my worst nightmare for the first time ever again — after tonight.

Maybe it won't be so bad. Going by myself means I'll be free to dance with tons of new, fun, interesting guys. (Not that there's anyone new left, but I guess you never really know.)

More important, I have an excuse to reward myself for my amazing courage — by buying myself a brand-new outfit!

CHAPTER
Staying on Top
10

"Where did you find that dress anyway?" Tia asked as Jessica finished filling the punch bowl. The dance committee had met here in the gym an hour ago to do all the last-minute setup stuff. "You look really great."

"Thanks," Jessica said, smiling. She glanced down at the peach slip dress and matching shrug she'd bought at the mall this afternoon. Mission accomplished. Not that looking good was all that mattered. But it couldn't hurt since Jade was almost definitely bringing Jeremy here, and Evan was taking Elizabeth.

And Jessica, of course, was here alone.

"I got it at Fashion Train," she added.

Lisa Lewis clapped. The sound echoed sharply in the almost empty gym. "People? People?" she yelled, her hands cupped around her mouth like a megaphone. "I still have a few more things on my list. We've got to hurry. The dance officially starts in just ten minutes." She motioned with her arms for everyone to gather around.

155

Jessica and Tia drifted across the shiny wood floor toward the group. They stopped next to Andy, forming a ragged semicircle facing Lisa.

Lisa frowned at her clipboard. "Okay, Jessica, nice job with the streamers. Could we just get a few more over by the snacks? Tia and John, Mr. Quigley needs help bringing in the rest of the soda from his car. Jamie and Scott, see if the band needs any help. The rest of you can finish arranging the chairs."

Andy held up a finger. "Excuse me? Exactly how should we *arrange* the chairs?" he asked, crossing his arms over his chest. "I mean, is there a standard homecoming style?"

Lisa's eyes widened in horror. The clipboard sagged in her arms. "W-What?" she stammered. Jessica sighed, wishing Andy could just give the poor girl a break. Her stress level was clearly through the roof.

Tia snorted and covered her mouth with her hand.

But Andy must have realized he was pushing Lisa too far because he immediately flashed a big smile. "I'm kidding, Lisa," he told her. "Don't have a stroke, please."

She glared at him, then thrust the armful of red streamers at Jessica. "These need to be taped up behind the refreshment table," she ordered. "Andy can help you," she finished, then walked away.

Andy lifted his shoulders and grinned sheepishly. Jessica laughed. "Come on."

She carried the streamers over to the table where she and Tia had been setting up the drinks a few minutes ago. Andy went to go grab the ladder, then followed her back to the table and helped her hang up the streamers. They were just taping up the last roll when the lights dimmed and the doors opened, letting everyone in. The band started up a fast song, but none of the people walking in moved onto the dance floor.

"I think we have to get things moving," Jessica told Andy. "Where'd your date go anyway?"

"Over there," Andy said, waving his hand at the opposite side of the room. Jessica looked where he was pointing and laughed when she saw her friend stuck in a conversation with a very tense Lisa Lewis.

"I think she needs rescuing," Andy said.

"Definitely," Jessica agreed. They set out across the room, coming up behind Tia in time to overhear Lisa's tirade about this song not having been approved by her when she saw an earlier version of the band's playlist.

"Tee, we need you," Jessica interrupted. She gave Lisa an apologetic smile. "Sorry," she said. "But don't worry—I'm sure everyone will love this song!"

Andy took Tia's hand and dragged her out to the dance floor with him and Jessica. The three of them began dancing in a group, and Jessica realized how lucky she was to have friends like Andy and Tia. She knew that even though they were technically each other's dates, they wouldn't leave her by herself. Maybe all the stress of the past week of planning and meetings would be worth it after all. Their senior homecoming could still be just as fun as she'd hoped.

She turned around to survey the crowd, relieved to see that more people had joined them on the dance floor. Lots of students were pouring in through the doors now—everyone with dates, of course. She studied each couple as they stepped inside, searching for someone else who had decided to come solo. She couldn't be the *only* girl without a date, right?

Suddenly she froze, her breath catching in her throat.

Jeremy. He stood in the doorway, dressed in black pants and that shirt she loved—a forest green polo shirt that showed off his lean, toned upper body perfectly.

He looked great, of course.

Jeremy took a step forward, and Jade appeared behind him, wearing skintight black leather pants and a ridiculously tiny tank top.

Jessica tore her gaze away, forcing her body to start moving again. Somehow her brain had gone into slo-mo when she'd caught sight of Jeremy, and she'd blanked on the reason he was here—to be with his *date*, Jade.

Deep breaths, Jessica told herself. She was

prepared for this. She could handle seeing them here together.

Yeah, right.

"Want to take a break?" Ken asked Melissa, bending down so that she could hear him over the pounding music. His lips were so close to her that his breath tickled her neck.

She grinned up at him and shook her head. They'd danced to almost every song the band had played since they got there, but she wasn't even slightly tired. She was having a great time—finally just being able to *relax* without worrying about everything. And Ken had been so nice too. He kept asking if she was hungry, thirsty, if she needed anything. And he'd turned down every pathetic wannabe who'd tried to dance with him. It was amazing the way all the girls there looked at him now that he was the new football star. But the best part was how they looked at *her*—the girl he was ignoring them for.

Which was the entire point of all of this.

She frowned as she thought about the only bump in the plan. Cherie, Gina, and her other friends had shot her some pretty weird glances when she walked in with Ken. They were obviously wondering what was up with Will—meaning she'd have to come up with an explanation.

I can deal with that later, she thought. For now she was just going to enjoy the success of this night.

"Why don't we get something to drink?" Melissa suggested. Ken nodded and took her hand to guide her through the crowd over to the refreshment table. Seth Hiller stood at the edge of the dance floor with Josh Radinsky, drinking their sodas. They both stared at her and Ken as they passed by, and Melissa felt another twinge of worry. What would Will's good friends think of this? What would they say to Will?

If Will even answers their phone calls. The way he'd been treating her, she seriously doubted he was staying in touch with anyone else.

"Check out the quarterback groupie," Seth said loudly right as Melissa walked by.

Melissa stiffened but kept her face blank.

Josh snorted. "Yeah. Bet she knows how to receive a pass." He glared at Melissa, and she felt herself blush. Luckily it was too dark in the gym for anyone to notice.

Ken's hand tightened around hers, and he jerked her back in the other direction, away from Will's friends.

"Sorry about them," Ken muttered as they walked over to an empty area by the wall.

"It's not your fault Will hangs out with jerks," she told him.

"So . . . do you want to leave?" he asked, shifting from one foot to the other. He glanced at her almost shyly, his blue eyes flicking over her face nervously.

"What? No, of course not." She inhaled deeply. "Why should we leave because of them?"

Ken shrugged. "Not because of them," he said. "For you—I mean, if you're not comfortable."

She smiled, realizing that he'd actually leave his own homecoming dance just for her, a girl he barely knew. Again he had managed to put her first when her own boyfriend couldn't.

The band started a slow song, and Melissa stepped closer to Ken. "Let's dance," she said softly, staring up into his eyes.

Ken smiled, then reached out and took her into his arms, slowly pulling her toward him. She laid her cheek against his gray dress shirt, swaying gently to the music. Their bodies seemed to fit together perfectly as he held her close, his hands resting comfortably on her lower back. It felt so natural. It felt . . .

Like it does with Will.

She swallowed, and beads of sweat formed on her palms. She and Ken had come here as friends, a football player and a cheerleader who both needed dates for homecoming. But now that she was dancing so close to him, even getting a whiff of his clean, guy scent—soap mixed with aftershave—her body was *not* responding in a purely friend way. She tilted her head up to his, and he was staring down at her, his eyes slightly glazed over. His face inched down closer to hers, and for a second she was convinced he was going to kiss her.

The thought sent a delicious shiver down her spine.

But just then the song ended, breaking the spell. Ken's expression cleared, and he pulled back from her, clearing his throat.

"Why don't we get those drinks now?" he said.

"Yeah, sure," Melissa agreed. She laced her fingers through his, this time leading him across the gym to the refreshment table. She didn't even care if they walked by Seth and Josh again.

She wasn't doing anything wrong. Not considering how Will had been treating her, at least. She'd asked him—no, *begged* him—to let her help, to let her come see him. And all he'd done was snap at her and then humiliate her.

Glancing back at Ken as they made their way through the couples on the dance floor, Melissa felt a strong sense of satisfaction. Ken was definitely interested in her—she could see it all over his face. His very *cute* face—the one attached to an equally nice body. If staying on top meant hooking up with him, then she wasn't really facing such a rough task.

"Hey, Jade, want to dance?"

Jeremy backed up as the tall, stocky Sweet Valley football player elbowed right past him to get to Jade.

Jade let her eyes travel slowly up and down the guy's body. Then she flashed a big, flirtatious grin. "Sure, Matt."

"Cool." Matt smiled back and led her out onto the dance floor, completely ignoring Jeremy. Maybe because it was kind of tough to figure out that Jeremy *was* Jade's date since she'd been busy dancing with just about every other guy there.

"I'll be back soon," Jade called out to Jeremy as she disappeared with Matt.

He shook his head, wondering why Jade had even bothered to invite him. She'd already danced with pretty much all of Sweet Valley's offensive line.

Jeremy rubbed a hand over his face. When he'd picked her up, Jade had been warm and friendly, like nothing was wrong. She still didn't say a word about those cards they'd given each other last weekend. He could only guess that she'd written his in some weird sentimental mood and then instantly regretted it after giving it to him, so now she was going out of her way to make it clear that she hadn't meant it. Ever since they'd walked into the gym together, Jade had been acting so crazy. She'd dragged him out onto the dance floor for the first dance, but after that, she'd said two words to him, and those were "no, thanks" when he'd offered to get her a soda.

Jeremy glanced out at the dance floor, searching for Jade and Matt. A fast song was playing, but they were dancing up against each other, their bodies almost touching. Then Jade leaned her head even closer to his, bringing her mouth to his ear to whisper something. Whatever it was, Jeremy could see

Matt's face turning crimson even from halfway across the gym.

Embarrassed, Jeremy quickly looked away. Maybe it was time to be honest with himself—things with Jade just weren't working. And it wasn't just the fact that he couldn't tell from one second to the next what she wanted. He'd been lying to himself when he thought he could make this casual-dating thing work. He wasn't that type of guy. He and Jade were just too different, and that was more obvious than ever tonight.

He thrust his hands into the pockets of his pants, then turned away from the dance floor, heading over to the exit. Would Jade even notice if he took off? She could probably catch a ride home from one of the million other guys she was dancing with.

But he was too nice a guy to ditch her like that, even after the way she'd ignored him tonight. That was his problem, really. He was too *nice*. Jeremy sighed, peering around the room for familiar faces.

Faces. As if there wasn't exactly one person he was looking for. He knew Jessica had been on the planning committee for the dance—she'd told him about it at House of Java last week. So she had to be here. With a date, probably.

Probably? Try definitely, he thought. As if Jessica Wakefield wouldn't have a hundred guys wanting to take her to the dance. And whoever Jessica's date was, he would bet that *she* was actually dancing with him.

Andy Marsden

<u>Homecoming-Dance</u> <u>Etiquette</u>

1. Do not linger in front of the refreshment tables, chowing down like you haven't eaten in a week. Unless you're a varsity lineman. Then it is permissible to hang out in front of the snack table with your fellow linemen, preventing others from gaining entry. This way you can scarf all the stale tortilla chips yourselves since you aren't dancing much anyway.

2. Slow dancing is just that—dancing. Two bodies plastered together from forehead to toes is not dancing; it's disgusting. Get a room.

3. Finally, a word of advice: When on the dance floor, do not attempt moves you do not have. That hip-hop step you saw on MTV last week doesn't look good when you do it. Believe me on this.

CHAPTER
No Regrets
11

A sharp lump rose in Jessica's throat as she watched Jeremy standing all by himself in the gym, looking so lost. She'd watched while Jade danced with everyone *but* her date, wondering why Jeremy was putting up with it. And why would Jade bring him here and then just abandon him like that?

". . . still think we should have all worn Real Men Play Rugby T-shirts," she heard Andy say. She, Andy, and Tia were taking a break from dancing, standing under the basketball hoop together while Andy shared all his amusing commentaries on the dance.

"Jess? Hello, you there?" Tia said, waving a hand in front of her face.

Jessica frowned. "Yeah, sorry," she said. "It's just—what is Jade's deal? Is she *trying* to crush Jeremy completely?"

Andy and Tia shared a sympathetic glance, and Jessica sighed. "Yeah, I know, none of my business," she said, anticipating the lecture about to come from her friends. "But I'm sick of just watching her do this to him. I'll be back, okay? I'm just going to go make sure he's all right."

She spun around and took off before either of them could stop her since she knew they'd try. As she wove through all the whirling bodies on the dance floor, she tried to keep her eyes trained on the floor—just in case. She knew Elizabeth and Evan were here together somewhere. Luckily she hadn't spotted them yet, and she was hoping for a miracle that would allow her to get through the whole night without a run-in. She just had a feeling she'd really lose it if she saw them all cozied up to each other.

Once she got closer to Jeremy and caught another look at his expression, she forgot all about her sister and Evan. The muscles in his face were all tight and tense, and his warm brown eyes seemed sad.

"Hey, Jeremy," she called out as she approached.

He glanced up and met her eye, then smiled in relief. "Hey, Jess," he greeted her. He took a few steps forward to meet her halfway.

She gave him a friendly smile, wondering how to start this conversation. When she'd interfered in things between him and Jade before, it had only made him angry at her—and sent him right back into the cheating girl's arms. She had to make sure she was more careful this time.

"So, how's it going?" she asked. There was a neutral question.

Jeremy shrugged. "Um, actually—not great," he replied. "Where's, um, your date?"

Jessica flushed. "Back there," she said, giving a general wave toward the other half of the gym. She wasn't exactly lying—Andy and Tia were sort of her dates, and they *were* where she was pointing. There was no way she'd ever admit to Jeremy that she didn't have a date.

"Oh," he said, nodding. "So, don't you need to get back to him?"

She paused. She didn't want to look like the kind of girl who'd ditch her date, the way Jade had, but she also didn't want to leave Jeremy. "He's talking to some friends," she explained. She stared at him closely, narrowing her eyes in concern. "But you really don't look happy. Want to go outside and talk?" she asked, pointing over at the exit sign.

"Yeah, I guess," he said. "For a couple of minutes."

They walked outside together, and as soon as they stepped out of the gym, the cool night breeze swept over her, giving her goose bumps. She shivered, pulling the shrug tighter around her arms.

"Cold?" Jeremy asked.

"No, I like it," she said. She would have welcomed arctic temperatures if it meant the chance to be alone with him, away from all the noise and people inside.

Jeremy nodded and stared off at the cars in the parking lot. He seemed content just to be there with her, not saying anything. Jessica studied his profile under the yellowish streetlights. He looked wrecked.

All because of Jade dancing with those other guys. Her heart sank. He had to be pretty serious about her to get this upset.

And if she was a real friend, she'd do something to help—even if it tore her up inside. She'd find a way to make things work out for him with Jade. He'd gone back to the girl even after he'd seen her kissing Josh. If he could forgive that, he really had to like her a lot.

She'd had her chance with him, and she'd blown it. But he'd never stopped being a good friend to her—and she owed him the same.

Jessica took a deep breath. "So, what's up with you and Jade tonight? Did you guys have a fight or something?"

"No." Jeremy kept his gaze focused on the cars.

"Well, something's obviously going on," she pressed. "This doesn't exactly look like a date to me."

"Yeah, you're not the only one," he said. "I have no idea what's going on with her. She's been giving me some major mixed signals lately."

"Why don't you try talking to her?" Jessica asked, wondering if her tone gave away how much she hated saying those words.

He groaned. "I have been," he said. "She's been so busy this week, I didn't get to talk to her for more than five minutes. Until she invited me to the dance,

I was starting to think she didn't even want to see me anymore."

"But she *did* invite you," Jessica pointed out. "That has to mean something."

He shrugged again, glancing down at the cement.

Slowly she reached out and laid her hand on his sleeve. The warmth of his arm beneath the fabric reminded her of the way it felt to hold him, to be close to him. She drew back almost instantly. If she let herself go down that route, she wouldn't be able to do this—to push him toward someone she couldn't even stand.

"Look," she began. "I really think you should get your butt back in there and talk to her. Maybe Jade has some weird idea that you don't want to be here with her or something. Let her know you're upset, and things will probably be fine."

"I don't know. . . ."

"I do." She shoved gently against his chest. "Now, go. Find her and talk to her before the dance is over. I, um, I have to get back to my date anyway."

"Yeah, okay," he said. He didn't seem too hopeful—his frown hadn't gone anywhere, and his eyes were still droopy. But at least she'd tried to help—and maybe once he took her advice and confronted Jade, everything would work out. She couldn't believe she was actually hoping for that.

Will aimed the remote control at the TV and switched it off in disgust. The Lakers had blown a fifteen-point lead. Not that he'd been really watching anyway. He tossed the remote onto the coffee table next to where his bad leg was propped. He'd been trying to take his mind off the clock all night, but it wasn't working. Not even slightly.

The green digital numbers on the VCR were impossible to avoid. *Nine thirty-two.* Five minutes later than it was last time he looked.

The dance would definitely be crowded by now. He leaned his head back against the couch cushions and closed his eyes. Everybody would be getting psyched for the game tomorrow. He could picture his friends dancing, messing with each other, making comments about how they were going to kick butt.

Yep, the whole team would be there by now, partying like crazy. The thought twisted painfully in his gut.

It should have been *his* dance, *his* game.

Sick of feeling so much self-pity, he swiped up the remote and switched the television back on, changing the channel. A tiny, dark-haired woman was scraping the claw end of a hammer across the surface of a frying pan. "See?" she said, smiling into the camera. "This new diamondlike coating resists even the worst scratches."

He narrowed his eyes at the woman, noticing how she had a similar body to Melissa's—the same slender but somehow strong-looking build. Even her long, dark hair reminded him of his girlfriend.

Not that he hadn't been thinking about her all the time anyway. He knew how annoyed she must be that he hadn't picked up the phone when she called the other night. But it was driving him crazy to hear her go on about everything he was missing out on at school. Like homecoming. Here he was, missing the dance he'd looked forward to for years. And meanwhile Melissa was . . . . well, actually, she was missing the dance too.

Somehow that hadn't really entered his thoughts until right now. But if he wasn't there, then she wouldn't be either. She was probably lying at home, feeling as miserable as he was. He felt a stab of guilt and lunged sideways on the couch to grab the portable phone. He started punching her number, but halfway through he stopped, clicking the phone back off. After how he'd acted this week, she'd just hang up on him. And she deserved more than a phone call anyway.

"Mom," he called out, hoping she'd hear him from the kitchen. "Mom, can you drive me to the game tomorrow?"

There was a pause, and then Mrs. Simmons came running out into the living room, her expression eager. "Did you say you wanted to go to the game tomorrow?" she asked hopefully.

"Yeah," he said. "Can you take me?"

"Of course," she replied.

"Thanks." He leaned back against the couch,

picturing the look on Melissa's face when she saw him there tomorrow, knowing he'd dragged himself there just to support her. And for the first time since his accident, he felt a spark of hope.

Is this thing ever going to end?

Jeremy glanced down at his watch. After he'd come back inside, he'd actually made an attempt to find Jade, but he hadn't been able to locate her anywhere. He figured she must be deep in the center of the dance floor, and he wasn't going to try and make his way through all those other couples.

Especially since a big part of him didn't even really *want* to talk to her—not since he'd realized that it was pointless. He wasn't into it anymore, and obviously neither was she. But he hadn't bothered explaining that to Jessica since she seemed suddenly obsessed with him working things out with Jade.

Talk about a turnaround. Just weeks ago Jessica was doing all she could to break them up, and now she was pushing him toward her. What was her deal?

Jeremy shook his head. He turned and walked over to the refreshment table, squeezing around a couple of girls to grab some chips. Somehow everything Jessica said outside had only upset him more. Now that he was convinced he and Jade were over, why did she want them to stay together so badly? Was the idea of Jeremy being single *so* unbearable to her?

He ran a hand through his hair, trying to calm down. Jessica had only been trying to help. She was a good friend. He knew that. Maybe her actions got a little out there sometimes, like when she'd dragged him to the beach to see Jade cheating on him, but her motivations were always well-meaning. And this time there was definitely nothing manipulative about what she'd tried to do. So why was it getting to him so much?

He shut his eyes for a second, trying to block out the answer. But it was there, obvious as anything. There was only reason it would bug him like this that Jessica wanted him to be with someone else—it meant she *didn't* want him to be with her.

And maybe he still wanted that more than he'd realized.

Elizabeth grinned as she watched Evan throwing his body into the fast hip-hop tune playing. His movements were perfectly in time to the beat, and she almost had trouble keeping up with him. Even in Birkenstock sandals, the guy was a decent dancer.

He dances like he does everything else, she thought, shaking her hair out of her face. *With endless energy and enthusiasm.*

Some guy dancing next to her jabbed her in the side with his elbow, and she winced, reaching down to rub her waist.

Noticing the minicollision, Evan reached for her hand and pulled her backward through the knot of dancers to a wider space on the floor. Before letting go of her hand, he pulled her close and whispered, "Just like the Riot without the smoke, huh?"

The feel of his breath against her ear made her shiver, and she felt her muscles tighten.

"I think the music's a little better there," she replied, raising her voice so he could hear her.

Evan laughed, and they started dancing again. She tried to relax as she moved to the music, letting herself get lost in the rhythm. It wasn't hard to do—being around Evan was so amazingly easy and fun. So . . . not *complicated*.

A flash of peach caught Elizabeth's eye, the same shade as the dress she'd seen Jessica wearing when she left the house earlier. She squinted and realized that it *was* Jessica, dancing with Andy and Tia.

Elizabeth immediately glanced away, hoping Jessica hadn't seen her looking. They hadn't come face-to-face all night, luckily. She would have been completely humiliated if Jessica had laid into her in front of Evan. It hurt that her sister still wasn't talking to her, but she couldn't twist herself around just to please Jessica. Or anyone else. Tia had managed to get past the Evan thing, and Jessica would too—sometime.

"This is it, Sweet Valley," the band's lead singer's voice boomed over the speakers. "Last dance. Let's take it slow."

At the first chord Evan held out his arms. He slid a hand to the small of her back and pulled her against him. She didn't resist—letting herself be wrapped up in his embrace. They swayed together to the music, Evan holding her tightly. She rested her cheek against his chest.

This is what having a boyfriend should be like, she thought. *Fun, uncomplicated . . . romantic.*

She closed her eyes, enjoying the feeling of Evan's warm body so close to hers, letting him guide their steps. Then suddenly he stopped. She glanced up at his face, confused. He was smiling down at her, his eyes so soft and caring.

Then he put a finger under her chin, tilting up her face until their eyes were locked together. Everything around them melted away, and she let him draw her even closer. Their lips were inches apart, and the tension in her body was overwhelming. She wanted him to kiss her more than she'd ever known.

When his lips met hers, an electric jolt shot through her. He kissed her lightly at first, waiting for her to respond.

For an instant Elizabeth blocked out the sensation as she remembered where they were—in the gym, in front of all their friends, all of Conner's friends. In front of Jessica.

But it didn't matter. She wanted this. She deserved this.

After a second's hesitation she leaned into him, wrapping her arms around the back of his neck, and kissed him back. No regrets. Not this time.

WILL SIMMONS
10:24 P.M.

$Will - football + Melissa = X$

$X = my\ new\ life$

CONNER MCDERMOTT
10:36 P.M.

So, here I am. At least I'm not in the car with my mom anymore. I was sure she'd get sick of saying Elizabeth's name, but it just didn't seem to happen during that entire trip here. She needs to get that things are over with us. And I'm fine with that. Completely fine.

JEREMY AAMES

10:38 P.M.

I wish this song would end. Of course Jade finally finds me to dance together now, for the one song that Jessica and I listen to when we close up at HOJ. Mmmm, she always looks so cute when she's wiping down the counter, making sure every single crumb is gone. Maybe I'll just close my eyes and pretend I'm dancing with Jessica instead. . . .

JESSICA WAKEFIELD

10:38 P.M.

Jeremy looks happy. Damn.

You'll always remember your first love.

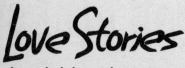

Check out the **all-new**....

..... (Sweet Valley Web site—)

www.sweetvalley.com

New Features

Cool Prizes

The **ONLY** official Web site!

Hot Links

(.... And much more!)

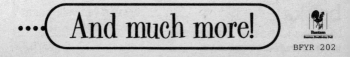

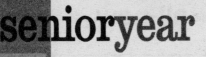